# The Martian Wave
## September 2024

### Short Stories
- 12    Perch by Eric Del Carlo
- 37    Shakespeare's Garden by James Arthur Anderson
- 48    A Cloud on Fire by Jason Lairamore
- 64    The Gray Area by Travis Lee
- 82    And So On Down the Drain by Eric Del Carlo

### Poems
- 36    Eunomian Scrapyard by Lee Clark Zumpe
- 47    Our Last Ice Giant Exploration by Lauren McBride
- 63    Watch Where You Step by Lauren McBride
- 99    Gunships Over Ganymede by Lee Clark Zumpe

### Illustrations
- 33    The Corridor by Denny Marshall

# THE STAFF OF THE MARTIAN WAVE

EDITOR: Tyree Campbell
WEBMASTER: H David Blalock
COVER DESIGNERS: Marcia A. Borell, Laura Givens

All rights reserved. No part of this book may be reproduced or transmitted in any form or by any means, electronic or mechanical, including photocopying or recording or by any information storage and retrieval systems, without expressed written consent of the authors and/or artists.

*The Martian Wave* is a work of fiction. Names, characters, places, and incidents are products of the authors' imaginations. Any resemblance to actual events or persons, living or dead, is entirely coincidental.

Story and illustration copyrights owned by the respective authors.

First Printing September 2024
Hiraeth Publishing
http://hiraethsffh.com/
@HiraethPublish1

Cover art by Richard E. Schell
Cover design by Laura Givens

Vol. V, No. 2                                      September 2024

The Martian Wave is published two times a year on the 1$^{st}$ days of March and September in the United States of America by Hiraeth Publishing, P.O. Box 1248, Tularosa, NM, 88352. Copyright 2024 by Hiraeth Publishing. All rights revert to authors and artists upon publication except as noted in selected individual contracts. Writers and artists guidelines are available online at www.hiraethsffh.com. Guidelines are also available upon request from Hiraeth Publishing, P.O. Box 1248, Tularosa, NM, 88352, if request is accompanied by a self-addressed #10 envelope with a first-class US stamp. Editor: Tyree Campbell.

# A Little Help, Please

In the world of the small indie press we fight a never-ending battle for attention to our work, as writers and in publishing. Here's an example: big publishers [you know who they are] have gobs of $$$ that they can devote to advertising and marketing. Here at Hiraeth Publishing, our advertising budget consists of the deposits for whatever soda bottles and aluminum cans we can find alongside the highways. Anti-littering laws make our task even more difficult . . . ☺

That's where YOU come in. YOU are our best promoter. YOU are the one who can tell others about us. Just send 'em to our website, tell them about our store. That's all. Just that.

Of course, we don't mind if you talk us up. We're pretty good, you know. We have some award-winning and award-nominated writers and artists, plus other voices well-deserving to be heard [not everyone wins awards, right?] but our publications are read-worthy nevertheless.

That number once again is:

www.hiraethsffh.com

**Friend us on Facebook at Hiraeth Publishing**
**Follow us on Twitter at @HiraethPublish1**

Annae (real name Maryjade) is an assassin sent to Deege, a forested world, to kill a plant and bring back the druzy who carries it. Druzies resemble young girls, but seem to have no life and no purpose but to act as transportation to the plants. In the process, Annae loses contact with her own spacecraft and is marooned on the world.

The man who hired Annae for this task is also responsible for the death of Annae's twin sister. Annae has accepted this contract because it presents an opportunity to kill the killer. However, the loss of the twin has crippled Annae. She is virtually unable to communicate with anyone, except in the course of negotiating her contracts. She has taken to talking with the memory of her dead sister, and with no one else.

Now, marooned on Deege, she must find a way to break out of her isolation and communicate with the druzies, and with a strange young woman who cannot speak, or she will be compelled to remain on this world forever.

https://www.hiraethsffh.com/product-page/becoming-jade-by-tyree-campbell

# What???
# No subscription to
# The Martian Wave??

## We can fix that . . .

The Martian Wave is published three times a year, in March, July, and November.  It contains science fiction, fantasy, and some dark fiction short stories, poems, articles, reviews, and art, mostly centered on the exploration and settlement of other worlds.  We offer one- and two-year subscriptions.  Go to the link below and order.  Simple.

https://www.hiraethsffh.com/product-page/martian-wave

## And remember:  a subscription makes a great gift, for a holiday or birthday or any time of the year!

## Pyra and the Tektites

Pyra, age thirteen, is running away from home in the Asteroid Belt because she's not doing well in school. Her parents want to send her to Mars for school, and she doesn't want to go. She sneaks aboard a cargo shuttle, and falls asleep in the hold. When she awakens, she finds herself in free-fall; the shuttle has been seized by the Tektites, a group of rebel pirates—

. . . and the adventures begin!

https://www.hiraethsffh.com/product-page/pyra-and-the-tektites-by-tyree-campbell

# The Sisterhood of the Blood Moon
## By Terrie Leigh Relf

For thousands of Earth years, the Transgalactic Consortium has had an invested interest in this planet and its inhabitants, the Haurans. While the Sisterhood of the Blood Moon and the Guardians work together with the Consortium and Haurans to restore balance to the universe, the Blood Moon is fast approaching. The power of this moon reveals untold secrets . . . including the sacred covenant with the Mora Spiders. There is an ancient pact that continues to be honored – but at what cost and for whose purpose?

The world may come to an end. But will there be a chance for a new beginning? And if so, where?

https://www.hiraethsffh.com/product-page/sisterhood-of-the-blood-moon-by-terrie-leigh-relf

# INDIGO
## By Tyree Campbell

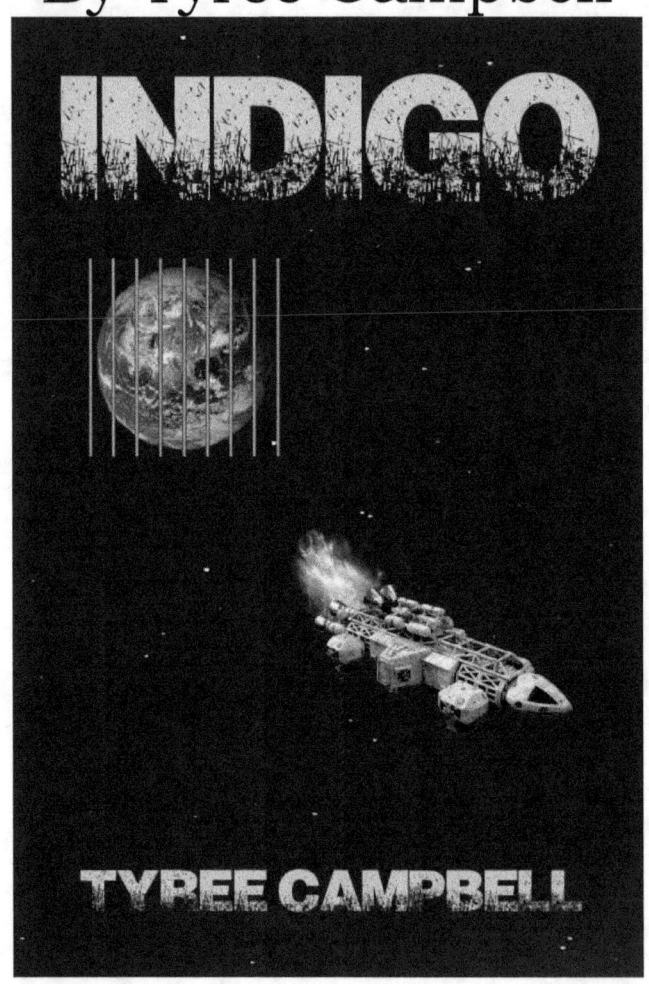

Matt has a special gift that will enable him to avenge his brother's death. Kerise has another use for that talent, if only she can persuade him to abandon his personal quest and help her with a project called Indigo.

Echelon, a secret government project, also wants Matt because of his gift. But as he and other like him cannot be controlled, they pose a threat to national security. Orders go out to have them eliminated.

Interpol is on the lookout for Kerise and for the Indigo project. There is no place on Earth where Matt and Kerise and her associates will be safe. Nowhere on Earth…but they cannot be safe unless Matt commits himself to Indigo. And he's not about to do that…

https://www.hiraethsffh.com/product-page/indigo-by-tyree-campbell

# Perch
## Eric Del Carlo

*He flies over gnarled blue-gray forest. He flies over the sprawls of meadows. He flies above deep jeweled lakes, swollen with icy runoff. He flies and avoids updrafts; he flies and uses a hardy updraft to lift him, which brings a rush to all his extremities. He flies in the thin cool greenish broth of the sky. He flies with verve, with precision and then with deliberate carelessness. He flies because there is joy in it. He flies for a purpose, separate from elation. And finally he flies for the no-reason, the primal urge. He is a thing of the free air, and here he must beat his glorious wings and carry his hollow-boned body over the slow, stubborn, terribly* anchored *land....*

*So, too, does he fly over the curiosity. The stranger. The...visitor?*

*Flies in a firm straight line directly over it, yet out of any possible reach. Because who knows what this is. Is it dangerous? Is it just another land-bound animal? He's never seen its like.*

\* \* \*

Maarne Simar watched the avian go over her head. She did not blink. She watched with her naked eyes, knowing devices--a battery of them--were recording this latest appearance. And its nearest appearance; it had never swooped over her so deliberately. For this *was* deliberate, wasn't it? It passed over in a straight line. She felt its shadow hit her eyeballs for an instant, then the avian was winging at easy great speed over a crest of stony hills.

She let out her breath, even as a flame-tongue of thrill continued to lick her innards.

Her sensory gear had no doubt just scored the best input yet. Superhigh-rez images, in a frame by frame breakdown, waited in her crystal-files. Her analyses programs would chew on the footage and give her exacting detail. She would know the flier's mass, its airspeed, the ligature which held those wings to the sleek downy body.

Of course she knew all that already. Because she knew the avians of this world. The planet was Graem; and the Graem people, an advanced race, had left behind a great deal of their civilization, including comprehensive anatomical and physiological data pools.

But this lone airborne being...was it purely of that fallen species? Or had it survived by becoming something else, by evolving into something more?

Maarne Simar shook her head and smiled, both gestures meaningless--she felt only dazed, at the moment--and went back into her sterile humming pod.

The straight line of flight. A conscious geometrical path, surely.

She had always admired straight lines. The straight lines of her life. The machined columns that marked her education, her introduction into her chosen profession, and the flourishing of that career.

Yet...

The angle had come, the divergence; and now she was here on Graem, a lone human visitor, studying not ruins--not the bones of collapsed cultures, as she'd trained ardently to do--but these last stray survivors of a not quite extinct species. Avians. The final feral remnants of the living civilization.

The change in career trajectory had caught her superiors unawares.

"Simar...are you quite serious about this?"

"I feel I can make a contribution to this study."

"But it's not really your field. Is it?"

"If no sentient life had survived there, I would be going, wouldn't I? To examine the relics."

"But some *did* survive. Are you sure about this?"

"I believe I can further the study."

Round and round like that. Until they gave in. And now she was here.

Inside the temperature controlled pod she turned to her equipment and set the direction and parameters of the analysis of the avian, then left the gear to its complex initial digestions. She pulled on a purple thermal coat and went back out. She straddled the wheeled mount and awoke its engine. The air was crisp in her lungs as she set off.

Roads had existed here, even among this airborne society. The avians--the Graemites--had moved bulky raw materials on the ground. The vehicles were hulks, with six huge wheels and gigantic beds. Maarne had already found several, fleshy vines from the surrounding forests engulfing them. She could infer their lumbering movements, the stately utile progress they must have made along the road system. But she did wonder what they had *sounded* like. Did they once growl like leviathans? Trumpet as mastodons? Was the might of their passage so great one felt it in one's marrow?

Now the roadways were overgrown, of course, but she could still make her way. She worked her mount's throttle, eyes flashing intermittently toward the sky. She had been seeing the same avian, over and over; she was certain; and now she would know him in detail, in scientific specificity.

Meanwhile, she would visit the nearest aviary once more.

She flattened grasses for a kilometer and pulled up in the rusty shadow of the imposing structure. A chill wind blew against her face. The aviary stood well off the ground, sculpted into a mountainside of matte gray rock, the lowest chambers some thirty meters above where she now stood. When she'd first found it--thrilled by her discovery--eagerness had made her try to scale the outer rock, to reach the yawning apertures where, once, no doubt, avians had flown in and out at will.

But she wasn't an able climber and kept reaching places where there were no further handholds. There was a flypack back at the pod, of course, but she didn't have the nerve to try it out.

At last, after determined but almost frantic searching, she had found a door in the base of the cliff; beyond it, corkscrewing stairs. She went up these same steps again now, until she came out into the bottom chamber. Here were the fairly preserved remains of the Graemite civilization, a great room loaded with lifeless technology. Liquid screens dominated a smooth stony wall, the surfaces still, dead, but suggesting a past when they had moved and flowed with purpose. Banks of other apparatus decorated the space, and plugged into these silent machines Maarne had found the cubes of data she had been able to unlock with her own equipment in her pod. Through these the avian civilization, in its day-to-day functionality, had revealed itself to her.

She knew how to interpret, to extrapolate, to reverse engineer. She learned how the social order had operated. She saw how the race understood itself. This, after all, was her field: societal deduction of dead communities.

Wind blew into the chamber, and she sank herself deeper into the thermal coat. The whole outer face of the room was open to the outside. No glass, no bars.

They had come through here, in bursts of flexing wings; and they had tended this equipment, and interacted, and done their work, and perhaps complained and laughed and carried on in all the natural informal ways of most peoples everywhere, throughout the galaxy.

Maarne could almost hear the dim echoes of their conversations.

She went up another set of steps and paced about in a higher chamber. Here a large section of the floor was clear, but symbols were drawn on it, overlapping ovals in different hues. Her guess was that a game of some sort was played here, a sport. But she had not investigated too deeply. Up. Again. To the next highest series of rooms. The gray mountain was tall, a rough upthrust of land, and it had been carved and hollowed all the way to the summit. Maarne climbed, pausing to look out from the gaping apertures, gazing out on vistas of blue-gray, the tangled forests; feeling a sweet rush of vertigo. She wasn't especially good with heights. It was one of the reasons she was hesitant about the flypack, though she had qualified to use it.

Up further she went.

This wasn't the sole aviary on the world, but it was the only one she had visited in the flesh. Before landing her pod, she had made an orbital scan; not the painstaking surveying she would have conducted had she come to Graem to undertake her more usual research procedures, which would have meant weeks of scrutinizing the surface with sensors from on high, but enough of a perusal of the land to know that the Graemite civilization had been widespread. And sophisticated. And fecund.

But they had fallen, nonetheless. That they were not extinct was probably something closer to a happy accident than any preplanning or deep-seated virtue on the part of the airborne species. They had collapsed themselves; it had happened roughly a century ago, according to the initial survey of this world, confirmed by Maarne's own first-blush findings while in orbit.

She breathed truly chill air into her lungs now. The wind sang into the chambers. She had reached industrial and administrative levels of the aviary, as empty as all the strata below. Outside, the greenish sky was flat and hard. It was a decidedly precipitous drop from these windows. Unbidden, her imagination gave her a sensation of falling and wheeling through the air, she a land creature with no hope of riding the air currents, bones too dense, limbs too clumsy, not made for the majesty of flight. Falling. Plummeting. Dropping inexorably toward an impactful death. Brief, catastrophic pain; then, nothing.

Reaching the levels which had once been living quarters, she was as struck by the warm aesthetics as the first time she'd climbed this high up the structure. The walls were painted with cartwheels of pastel color. The effect was beyond artistic. Her very skin seemed to respond to the splashes and circles of hues. The interconnected chambers radiated a lovely homeyness. Here was a place which was safe, her senses told her, where there was comfort and fellowship and decided security in numbers. Surely these rooms had flocked with inhabitants. There were rubbery slings strung everywhere, hundreds and hundreds of them; and these, Maarne intelligently conjectured, had served the avians as beds. The material was durable, pliant, but beginning finally to decay.

Yet the notion of this uppermost level of the carved out mountainside as a dwelling place, an area to rest in, overcame her with great psychic force. She wandered among the curious hammocks, touching this one and that, making them sway a little, and she shivered with a vision of these rooms filled with the Graemites at the peak of their power and refinement, with their society functioning at optimum efficiency. Her eyes drifted shut, and she drew long trembling breaths into herself. The fantasy grew in her, until it felt like memory or revelation: the beings soaring in and out, coming in off the crisp plane of the outside air, wings beating, downy bodies flexing, full of the life of their kind, alive in perfect concert with the sky, aware of the safety of this place, of the whole sprawling assured web of civilization covering this world of theirs. They had dominion here. They were the apex species. They enjoyed a technological order; their machines were capable, their tools deft, their computers able. But they remained creatures of the wind; and there was joy to be had in undulating their bodies through the vault of the sky, exercising their primal selves, performing over and over the simple sacrament of flight.

Maarne Simar heard now the cacophonous shushing of wings, five hundred pairs all at once. She felt on her chilled face the draught of those active feathery appendages. And for that time that her eyes remained closed, she felt the whole mountain teem with life.

\* \* \*

*He flies through his waking hours. He flies and he eats. Certain trees among the gray and blue sprawl of the forests produce a bulgy, spongy fruit in their high branches. It is easily graspable in his talons. When he bites into one, the juice is like a jolt and he happily consumes all the meat of the thing, dropping the pebble-textured rind when he is done. He flies into rain clouds with his mouth wide, and he drinks in gulping drafts. He flies while he voids wastes. He flies in his sleep, for his muscles move with clean efficiency and he is healthy and vital and driven by reflex. Always he is in flight, and this is his natural state; no other makes sense to him.*

*He flies and there are other creatures on the wind, smaller, darting, and he occasionally snatches one of these and bites into it. The winged animals have flavor, but he doesn't much like how they squirm and squeal before he can dispatch them, so he does not hunt much in his skies.*

*Rarely, rarely, he sees in the distance something which looks like himself. Wings beating in broad smooth strokes, body supple and trimmed with down. A shape soaring and swooping as he does. Always the sight sends vast alarm through his senses, and his blood pounds. He doesn't know if this is outright fear, but the sensations are so unnerving, so disquieting, that he turns away, veers off, and flies hard and fast away from the thing that looks like him.*

\* \* \*

Now she knew from her analysis that the winged being was male. No mistaking that organ nested among the downy pelt. She knew too that this was indeed a true avian, like all his bygone ancestors; not a mutant, not any evolutionary stray. He hadn't suddenly developed disaster-proof survival skills. He--his immediate progenitors, anyway, going back a few generations probably--had simply slipped through while the ultimate calamity was consuming the civilization on Graem. The avians had reached a fatal brimming point, and when societal safety measures had failed all at once, violence and disease had come crashing in, like a maddened tide. Such things happened. The native Graemites had had technology, but they hadn't reached beyond their own world. When the collapse arrived, they had nowhere to run.

Except a few, obviously, *had* fled.

Her initial sweep of the planet had shown a scattering of living inhabitants, a pitiful number; not enough, surely, to restart the species. Normally Maarne Simar wouldn't come to such a world where life was still stirring, even in these vanishingly small quantities. She dealt in ruins, in dead cities, in the inert carcasses of onetime proud cultures.

But the straight line of her life had diverged, and now she was studying survivors instead of the apparatus and monuments and effects a gone people had left behind.

Studying *one* survivor, anyway. She sat in her antiseptic pod and examined all her data. She was sure it was a single individual who had been "visiting" her. The avian had circled at a distance for days, then yesterday had made that dramatic swoop over her position, as if to say: I am here, you are there, I am aware of you.

Maarne sat back from her cool glowing screens. Was she becoming fanciful? Did she mean to project human responses onto the doubtlessly untamed avian? It was no way to conduct a composed, competent study.

She gazed awhile more at the readouts.

Finally she realized there was nothing more she could do on the ground.

* * *

Control was in the hips. There lay the balance point. It seemed counterintuitive, however, and Maarne had to deliberately resist the panic-urge to flail her arms. It was one thing to qualify to work a flypack on a training grounds; something else to strap it on out here alone, without supervision.

She couldn't wear her favorite thermal coat, of course, but she scrolled the thick flexible flysuit onto her body. She wondered idly how she would stand up to the sensor scrutiny she'd given her avian friend. She was aged forty-two in homeyears; she was short, somewhat compressed, but with a sturdy musculature and good skeletal structure. Perhaps she was even attractive by the standards she remembered. Her career had taken her far and wide, to many worlds; but anyone who had a purpose could be folded through space to undertake important missions.

It had left little time for courting, for romance, for family. Yet she imagined herself a family, nonetheless: a fancy of younger days, one she'd held onto into her grim but fulfilling middle years. A husband. A child. No, two children. They even had names. Married to Lyd, strong, handsome, not quite her intellectual equal but far more adroit with his emotions, lavishing love upon her; and the little ones, Beck and Harrow, younglings, little loves, all curiosity and wonder and warmth....

She was up off the ground, feeling the deep marrow drone of the flypack's impellers. Hips. *Hips.* She scolded herself, forcing memories of her training to the forefront of her brain. No time to think about anything else, much less an imaginary family.

In the air she overbalanced, performed an unintentional somersault, and concentrated harder. There. A little better. There. Better still. She hovered, well off the turf. Her vertigo encroached, and she let it. This was simply something she would have to get used to. She'd set her pod down in a meadow of greenish-blue grasses, the blades thick. If she plunged to the ground, she would survive the impact.

She rose further, finding the proper feel for the impeller units. The air was cool on her exposed cheeks. Her eyes were covered over with goggles, and these were equipped with distance sensors. A few small birds were in the vicinity, but she didn't have the time to search all the heavens for her avian. Working the flypack occupied her fully. She executed rudimentary maneuvers. She started to feel a first real balance, deep within her body, that gyro point. After a time she could wriggle and shimmy with increasing subtlety, and she would bank and soar as she wished.

It became exhilarating, then exhausting. She'd been up for hours now. She had used up the day learning to fly again, learning this atmosphere, on this world where she was the only human being.

When she at last alit, her muscles ached and the flysuit felt glued to her flesh. She reeled some on the ground, which suddenly seemed too solid underfoot, lacking all the grace of free space and flowing air currents. She grinned, the expression unusual on her rather stolid face.

She took a last look at the sky and its heavy emerald tones of sunset, and saw nothing moving up there. She clumped inside the pod and sealed the door.

\* \* \*

*When he sees the thing in the distance that looks like himself, he does as his instincts have taught him: he banks quickly about in a half circle and beats a course away.*

*But something disquiets him, and in his mentally unsophisticated way he examines the image in his memory. He is not one for scientific analysis. He knows on some level that he is young; but the concept of young isn't wholly clear to him. He has been on his own for as long as he can remember, and if, before, there was a time when this was not so, he harbors no memory of it. And so he continues deliberately in his alone state and avoids these airborne others he has occasionally seen in his continuous travels.*

*But...this most recent sighting? Something about it. Something.*

*It was about his size--but wrong. Where were the beating wings? The realization startles him. He knows his own endlessly undulating wings are what keep him aloft and in motion. It's the same for the lesser fowl he finds in his skies.*

*But if this strange other was without wings, it shouldn't have been able to fly at all--*

*...and yet it did.*

\* \* \*

It took two days of multiple two-hour stints in the sky--coming down to eat, to rest, to crouch with her head between her legs until the dizziness was once again all past--before her goggles picked him up. No doubt as to his identity; she had him mapped crest to talon, after all. His down was greenish, his wingspan impressive by the standards of his kind. Avians didn't really have humanoid faces, but they possessed enough features and facial mobility to give them a thoughtful, sentient range of expression.

Certainly this stray who'd taken such a helpful interest in her was possessed of sentience. But did he retain even a scintilla of avian culture? Maybe not. To survive, his forebears surely had had to cut themselves off from all society. Go rogue. Go savage. Avoid the violence and disease. This individual, then, would have been raised outside all civilized norms. If he'd been raised at all.

But now she had seen him, her goggles zeroing in, focusing, bringing her back an image. She had seen him fly before, of course, but how different it was to watch from this vantage, up here in his natural arena. He swooped across the green ether, beneath the chill wash of sunlight, graceful, robust.

She had been taking her flypack in a circle roughly a kilometer out from the pod. Perhaps he had seen her earlier, with keen avian eyes which were at least as good as the artificial eyes of her goggles. He might have spotted her and fled. What a clumsy beast she must make, gyrating through the sky, struggling still sometimes to keep her hips centered.

But now he lingered; at a distance, to be sure, but he was there in her line of sight. He appeared to be observing her. She had halted, was hovering. She put herself into motion once more. Let him see what she could do, even if she did it awkwardly.

And so she flew, and performed her somewhat labored aerial maneuvers. Her muscles had hardened in the past days, and she was used to the cold windburn on her face, the snug sweaty warmth of the flysuit and the cinching straps that held the flypack rig to her.

He began to move as well. He followed her course, still far-off, a tentativeness to his flight pattern. Soon, though, he flew with a growing fluidity. His natural grace returned. Maarne, consequently, tried to imitate *his* maneuvers, the sweep and roll of his flight. She had only the impellers to move her, while he sailed through the air on the strength and deftness of his magnificent wings.

They soared like that, well apart, but for something like fifteen continuous minutes. Then abruptly he winged off, heading for the horizon, and she did not pursue.

When she landed beside her pod, she was flushed with exertion and aglow with her accomplishment.

Whether or not she was legitimately fully qualified to undertake this mission, she was making progress. She had established sure contact with one of this planet's survivors. He wasn't a dead piece of the fallen Graemite civilization; he was living and vital, and she'd gotten his attention, for certain.

\* \* \*

*He goes to dance with the curiosity. He had trouble at first believing this was, in fact, the stranger, the odd upright land creature he has teased with lately. It doesn't seem to him that it should fly. But it does. It does.*

*They swoop together. He maintains an instinctual margin of safety. Yet that innate caution does not cause him to flee, as he would have if this were one who looked more like himself. That the curiosity is so bizarre allows him, perversely, to keep company with it.*

*It is very much not like him. No down, no wings. It moves...strangely. As if it weren't used to flight. Is this a youngling, even younger than himself, just learning the skies? It puzzles him. Where did it come from? The conundrums trouble his head. He isn't used to thinking like this.*

*He tries to live in the moment, which is how he has always conducted his life. Fly, just fly, forever flying; seeing to his necessities, eating and excreting and sleeping; and never coming down out of his sky, never resting the action of his wings.*

\* \* \*

Maarne Simar, body singing with a high sweet fatigue, crept inside her pod where she lived and worked. This was a physically taxing operation. She was spending as much of her waking hours in the air as on the ground. When night came, she quit the skies, spent yet invigorated. She didn't know where the avian went during the darkness.

She unbuckled the flypack and peeled off the flysuit. She felt limp. Her body wanted hot food and deep sleep, but she went to her research node instead, and sat and plugged in one of the data cubes she'd taken away from the empty aviary. Her screens glowed.

Here was the entirety of the avian culture, their ways, their knowledge. They'd been a recording people, for which Maarne was grateful. When she had first tapped this reservoir of information, it had been overwhelming, a deep encyclopedic mass. Now, after days of flying with her airborne companion, she had a focus, a place to center her inquiries. Fortunately the Graemites had not been squeamish about such things. The data she wanted was presented forthrightly, without blushing diffidence.

When she had what she wanted, she doused her screens. She prepared a hot meal and ate it. Hers was a lonely dinner table inside the pod, but she had the lingering fantasy of a family to keep her company if she wanted it, if she summoned it with enough force. Her husband, their two children. Lyd, Beck, Harrow.

After she ate, feeling warm and puffy and drowsy, she went briefly outside, pulling her purple thermal coat over her shoulders. She looked up at the stars, but she wasn't really observing the points of celestial light; rather, she watched for any interruption to those icy points of illumination, for anything passing between her gaze and the stars, something in the atmosphere, something in flight over the land.

And she wondered: did her avian *ever* leave these skies?

\* \* \*

*He takes the curiosity hunting. Not for the small fliers; he doesn't want to teach how to kill. Instead they go for the treetop fruit. The stranger in his sky has no talons, but on the ends of limbs there are...grabbing things. Such a weird animal. It still makes no sense to him that it can fly, but he's accepted it nevertheless.*

*He finds the proper trees and goes into a dive. He snatches the elastic spheroid, tearing it from its stem, and carries it off. Sometimes there are branch-climbing animals nearby the fruits, and they might try to lunge at him, but he has been too quick. He circles, demonstrating to the curiosity how to rend the pebbly rind to expose the juicy meat. When he finishes feeding, he gestures at the top of the tree, where other fruits await.*

*The curiosity hovers. Its head is odd, but it has eyes and a mouth and its face isn't that peculiar, he decides.*

*He watches the creature move in, much more cautiously than he. He takes in her shape, her size. Roughly his own length, though obviously differently configured. They fly fairly near one another now, just a few wingspans apart sometimes. He does not expect to be attacked but is ready to defend himself if necessary.*

*He wonders about the curiosity. The differences between them seem more profound than surface peculiarities. It is one more concept he can't quite express. Lately he's encountered a number of these troubling thoughts. He cannot remember his life being so disturbed before.*

*But he doesn't wish to flee. The stranger intrigues him. He wants to know more. Sometimes he hears remote echoes in his head, inexplicable sounds that maybe come out of his past. It is possible--just possible--that once he knew more than he does now, that he once received...instruction.*

*And it is out of these dim echoes that he unexpectedly snatches a term, an idea. It is at once a huge concept and a tiny notion, something utterly basic. Something, perhaps, he really should already know.*

*He wonders, as he watches the curiosity take a first bite of fruit, if this other is a female.*

\* \* \*

It was, in one view, a fool's errand she was on. She had come to Graem to study these last vestiges of a sentient species; but that race's fate was surely decided. Yet her mission included this optimistic imperative: aid these beings if she could.

A colossal task. Monumental. Beyond the scope of her abilities--or anyone's, really. She wasn't a god. She couldn't manipulate a whole people back to prosperity. She probably couldn't even rescue one of them, not even this one, to whom she had grown somewhat...close? Was that the right word? He was feral, to be sure. Without language. She'd tried out sounds on him, recordings from the Graemite archives, but he only appeared nonplussed--

if she was even reading his facial expressions correctly--when she played Graemite speech on a mobile device. At any rate he had never tried to duplicate the sounds, and she gave up her efforts.

She had seen what he ate. The fruit was quite tasty. He led her through the skies, passing over lakes and clearings and forests and hills. He seemed interested in her.

Their flights together were engrossing. She had never imagined herself engaged in such an animated activity before, even when she had entreated her superiors to give her this assignment. She'd thought she might go aloft once or twice, but nothing like this.

Perhaps there was even more to it, this congress they shared. Perhaps--perhaps--there was some... attraction? Did he find her appealing? A disconcerting notion, but one which didn't outright horrify her. Even more dismaying: was she drawn to him on even the most subtle level? The romanticism of flight, maybe. He might be akin to something out of human mythology, touching on some primeval desire in her. The winged man, the soaring demigod. And she, perhaps, wanting to lie with him...

She left these thoughts under-examined.

Now she tried to exert a little influence over him. He'd led her; she attempted to lead him. She banked and wanted him to follow. She had seen him use rudimentary gestures, and she tried these, waving him the way she wished him to go. She knew where she wanted to take him.

It was start and stop, forcing many frustrating efforts, but after a while he seemed to grasp the idea--or was at least willing to go along for a time. Her goggles were equipped with directional readouts. She guided him over the world's surface.

The range of matte gray rock came into view. Its precipitous face was hollowed out with level after level of chambers. It was the aviary she had explored several times, the site she would have ensconced herself in had this been a normal mission for her. Here were clearest impressions and detritus of the avian culture.

But she didn't intend to show him any of the accoutrements of his bygone people. She looked to him, holding his eyes a moment, then she dived slowly toward the uppermost chambers, to the wide open aperture of one. She alit on the outer ledge and turned to see him lingering behind, beating his wings uncertainly, like a wary swimmer treading water.

Excitement shook in her. She gestured broadly to the inside, to the friendly pastel colors on the walls, to the rubbery slings stretched everywhere. This could be the breakthrough moment. Perhaps he had some knowledge of this place.

His wings beat harder, snapping up and down, as he continued to hover in place. His down grew agitated, ruffling, and his left talon was opening and closing rapidly. It was the one he'd used to grab that fruit off the tree.

She peered closely, trying to read his features, trying also to offer him a calm and welcoming countenance of her own. This aviary had once been the seat of his people's society. This chamber wasn't just a living quarter; it was a place for breeding, for the starting of families. There were other avian survivors on this world, roaming its skies. Some of those were female. Her pod's sensors had told her as much.

But he came no nearer and still appeared distressed.

Maarne goosed her impeller units and wafted carefully toward him. She held her hands out and spread. She sought to communicate the warmth she felt toward him, something more than cool professional interest. She *wanted* him to survive, to live some kind of fulfilling life, even among the moldering skeleton of his native civilization.

When she was no more than a meter away, he spun suddenly into action. Both his talons flashed open, the hooked points gleaming dangerously in the sunlight, and he opened his mouth and shrieked at her--a loud, ferocious, dissonant cry. Nothing from the oral language of his ancestors. A raw scream of primitive violence.

She froze, fully expecting for the space of two fast swollen heartbeats to be torn apart in midair. This avian had the bodily strength to carry that out.

But instead he whipped in a semicircle. He shot away from her so fast that he was a distant point before she could even gather a decent breath. The goggles kept him in sight awhile, but he was racing away. And soon he vanished over the curve of the land.

Despondently she returned to the ledge. Fatigue ate at her--at her spirit this time. She had failed. Surely this was failure. She had thought she could lure him, that her femaleness might be enough. His reaction to the aviary had been almost phobic. She should have seen, perhaps even foreseen, his aversion. He wasn't a city dweller. He was a wild child. And now he would doubtlessly associate her with this forbidden place and avoid her at all cost.

Eventually she flew herself back to the pod. She was tempted to go on ground, but it was a long walk and she didn't have the motorized mount here. Still, she couldn't wait to get this damned flypack off. Very likely she would never put it on again.

\* \* \*

*He flies in fury, in uproar. There is no joy to his flight, no elation. He has seen...the bad place. Several like it exist. He has witnessed them, flown around them--always at a fearful distance. Those cliffs, with the strange caves on their faces. No. No! Bad places. Never go there.*

*Never. So say the echoes in his head.*

*He gasps. The long-elusive sounds. Suddenly he hears some snatch of them, a faint but coherent reverberation, and for the first time he understands what has dwelled in his memory for so long.*

*A warning. Avoid others. Avoid the gathering places especially. Danger there. Sickness. Violence. Death. Just fly. Fly and fly and fly forever...*

*Who told him this?*

*A...female? One with proper wings.*

*His...mother?*

*He does and does not know the word. It is a bloodless abstract, some nearly lost iota of knowledge. Another concept to make his head hurt.*

*The curiosity betrayed him!* His rage propels him onward. He flies blindly, savagely. How near he came to the bad place, close enough to actually peer inside. He'd been unable to stop himself. He *had* looked, going against the warning that had been planted deep inside of him, long ago.

But--the bad place had been empty. How could it have hurt him?

It feels like heresy to wonder this, even though "heresy" is another intangible he can barely wrap his unsophisticated brain around. Why is he so stupid?

Self-contempt adds to his fury. He is broiling with unfamiliar and unwanted emotions. Everything had been so simple before the wingless stranger had showed up.

He flies on. He is burning up a good deal of energy. He should eat or sleep or both. But he is too perturbed.

He soars over an expanse of forest. Probably he has flown over it before, at some point. He has ranged far across this world. That much he knows for certain. But the woods below have an effect on him. He feels a kind of invisible pull. The trees are dense and quite tall. This isn't the usual blue-gray woodland. Here and there, he sees, are spirals of arresting color, trees whose highest branches are circles of rich inviting hues. Soft oranges, gentle reds, tranquil yellows. These treetops are also decorated with some sort of substance. Curious, he glides lower. No tree-dwelling animal lunges up at him, and somehow he hasn't expected there to be any. In his skies he is untroubled by predators.

But the treetops enthrall him, so much so that he scarcely notices that his wrath has abated. The sting of betrayal has passed.

The high branches are strung with a dully glistening resin. He circles and circles, gazing with great curiosity. Finally he swoops low enough to pluck at a string with his talon. The substance is springy but firm, like nothing he has encountered before. The strands cross back and forth *among the branches, making a kind of web. A cradle. A...nest?*

*The word--the ghostly thought-idea--sends a thrill tingling through him. He is thinking again of the mother-word and what it might mean. Then he thinks beyond her. Her. Female. Yes, yes, could it be--*

*Still circling, a tightening spiral now. He is directly above the colorful circle made by the novelly colored foliage of the high resin-strung treetop.*

*He circles and circles. Strange powerful instincts working inside him, sending him urgent messages, guiding him. He does not feel the impulse to flee. Rather...the opposite.*

*Around he goes in a final quiet turn, talons just a whisper above the bed of resin strands.*

*Until, at long last, he alights. And slowly folds his wings at his sides. And rests. And begins to wait.*

\* \* \*

Depression wrapped her like a warm blanket. She felt listless, slightly nauseous. Lying on her bunk inside the pod, she gazed sightlessly at the ceiling.

Her "solution" to the avian problem had been both too modern and obsolete. She'd had it in her mind that by bringing her subject to the aviary she might touch off a latent memory or bit of lore or outright knowledge about the place, that it might spark in his brain that here he might congregate with others of his kind; hopefully with a female, and thus gain a long shot at preserving his species.

But her male avian would have known nothing of the functioning civilization which had produced the aviary and many others like it across the face of Graem. The aviaries were dead. She'd attempted to introduce him to the site, in hopes that against all odds a compatible mate might somehow show up and provide an answer to the question of imminent avian extinction. How could she be so stupid?

He had rejected the aviary. Rejected her.

She should have looked to the past, to historical rites and ways. When the avians didn't have roads and cities and mining and technology, when they had lived on the wind. And when they had done their courting and mating at the treetop level.

Her research had shown her how it was done: the brightly foliaged leaves at the tops of certain trees; the heavy sap of those trees; that resinous substance webbing the uppermost branches; and how the male would perch there, plucking at the strands until they made a pleasing pattern, and how a passing female might espy him and circle and trade guttural calls, and finally alight, and nest there with him.

*That* was the solution. But she had blown her chance.

Maarne closed her eyes. The depression was too familiar. She had felt its like before. It was a sense of engulfing futility, as though any- and everything she did was pointless, empty of purpose.

It hadn't been this way at the start of her career, when the line had been straight, before the divergence which had sent her to this world, evidently to fail. Then again, the line had diverted for a reason. The deep sadness she felt was at least somewhat justified.

Lyd. Beck. Harrow. They were not imagined; it was only that they *seemed* illusory now. Her family had, in fact, been the very one she had pictured for herself as a young woman. Somehow she had made the dream a reality. She had met Lyd, fallen in love with him, married him, and produced two superb children with him.

It was that rarest of accidents which had taken them: a fold-space mishap. Infinitesimally unlikely. A vanishing ghost of a possibility of it ever occurring to anyone traveling across the void of space. But it had happened to her three loved ones, who were coming to join her on a world while she studied its dead ruins.

Now the full weight of depression was on her again, as it had been in the immediate aftermath. It would sink her this time, permanently. Or...would it?

She opened her eyes.

There was something about her current mission, something that stirred her still, despite the day's failure.

Maybe she had irreparably scared off her primary subject. He might spend the rest of his life flying in endless circles through the green skies.

But--but there was yet something undeniably worthy in her overall goal. Study the avians. Help them. Guide a pair toward mating. Give the species even the narrowest chance. Yes. Yes. Worthy. Worthwhile. A noble effort.

And she could still do it. She could lift this pod and pilot it to some other part of the world. Find another avian. Or two. Strap on the flypack again, go up, befriend the natives. Find the right treetops, painted in the same pastels as in the aviary's breeding chambers. Encourage a male to roost, coax a female into his vicinity so that she might see him there. Hope that the primal instincts were intact, that nature would tell them both what to do.

She could make that effort. Couldn't she?

She would do it for her avian friend, the one she had failed.

She would do it in the name of her family's memory.

She would do it for her own survival. Because that mattered too.

Maarne grinned, pulled up the covers, turned on her side, shut her eyes again, and slept. And dreamed of having wings.

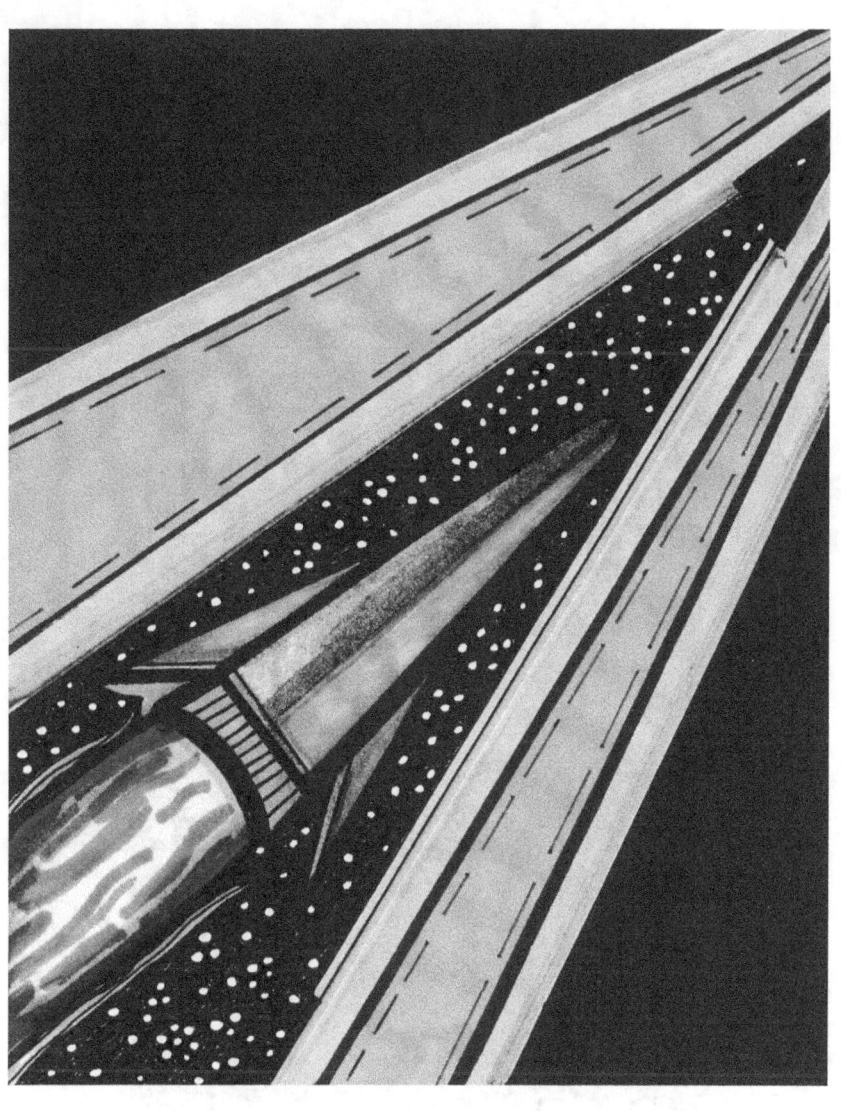

The Corridor
Denny Marshall

# The Spark
## By Stephen C. Curro

Katrina grew up in a frigid world ruled by a tyrant. By day, she works as a mechanic. At night, she becomes the Ace, the King's personal assassin. She's not proud of her job, but she's accepted that it's the way things are. At least she has her boyfriend Dez and his little brother Uriah to light her life.

When Katrina is ordered to quash a rebel attack on the King's Command Center, she thinks it's just another job. But as she uncovers the plot, she is shocked to learn that Dez may be involved with the dissidents. Now Katrina must make an impossible choose—eliminate the one she loves, or defy the King she swore to serve.

The Spark is a sci-fi thriller about love, betrayal, and how the futures of others, even a whole civilization, can be determined through a single choice.

https://www.hiraethsffh.com/product-page/the-spark-by-stephen-c-curro

# Eunomian Scrapyard
## Lee Clark Zumpe

I found her close to the barycenter
of the Eunomian family,
deep in the scrapyard,
surrounded by ancient debris;

I found her amidst scuttled frigates,
and decommissioned freighters,
fleets of obsolete short-range starfighters
spinning stubbornly through the implacable blackness;

I found her grounded on a stable asteroid
of siliceous mineralogical composition,
her hull intact, showing little battle scarring,
though stripped of her ion ultradrive engines.

I found her surprisingly easy to infiltrate –
scavengers had already picked her clean –
and spent hours roaming the icy corridors,
tracing my great grandfather's footsteps.

# Shakespeare's Garden
## James Arthur Anderson

Shakespeare's Garden was a tiny place, just four meters by eight, but to Christopher Berry it was the most beautiful place in the known universe. It would have been remarkable anywhere, but here in the barren landscape of Mars, under the cool glass dome of the city, it was breathtaking. Enclosed by an ivy-covered brick wall that shielded it from the rest of the city and trapped the fragrance inside, the tiny garden looked like an entire world of its own. It was an illusion of design, of course. No matter where one stood, beauty was all that could be seen. But the rainbow colors, the bouquet of varied fragrances, the soft bubbling fountain—that was no illusion.

Christopher sat on the stone bench and drank in the sights, the sounds, and the smells—the blues and yellows, and especially the delicious greens. He hadn't realized the beauty and rarity of green until he'd left earth.

He's come to the garden to read and relax and to think, as he often did. As a card-carrying member of the philosopher's guild, thinking was what he did for a living, and the garden was where he did his best work. But today, all he could think about was how soon this wonderful place would be gone. He pushed a stray lock of gray hair from his forehead and recalled yesterday's failed attempt to keep the garden.

He'd argued as long and eloquently as he could in the colony's assembly hall. He'd cited the ancients and the modern, from Plato's theory of aesthetics to Lennon-McCartney, to the Bard himself. But it was to no avail. The elders had been sympathetic. They had listened patiently, nodded appropriately, and considered the matter gravely. But in the end, it all came down to simple physics. The hard and cold fact was that a public garden —even a tiny one—was a luxury that this wasteland planet simply could not afford.

The problem was with the water. As the colony had grown, the water-producing machinery had been strained to the limits. Christopher had, of course, used the logic that the plants created oxygen in his arguments—but the elders had replied that food-producing crops also produced oxygen and with less water. No, the scientific argument failed, no matter how one looked at it. The garden existed for aesthetics alone and that was not enough to justify its existence.

Christopher looked around the garden and sighed. The world was devoted to science now—to technology and the pursuit of knowledge. And, most important, to survival. Food, shelter, water, oxygen—this was the currency of Mars, and of the universe, for that matter. Even the elders knew that the world had moved on. He and his garden were merely relics of the past, as much as the artifacts of the ancient Martian civilization that the archeologists studied, even now.

Unlike the ancient Martian civilization, though, this world had little use for his knowledge. Studying the extinct Martians might hold some key to survival, even if only to learn what had destroyed them. But no one seemed to have much use for a philosopher these days.

Commander Riley had said it best, even in his hard-edged candor.

"The only reason you're here is because guild regulations demand that each colony have a registered philosopher as part of its contingent," Riley had told him at his initial debriefing. "I have a colony to run and have no use for such things. So don't you for one minute forget your place here. I'd trade three of you for one good technician. Hell, I'd trade you for a mediocre one I could train. As far as I'm concerned, you're just a parasite. It's nothing personal, mind you. But I need people who can carry their own weight. And, frankly, philosophy isn't very high on the priority list right now."

Christopher had gone out of his way to avoid the commander after that, and though Riley had been polite to him in public, he had no illusions about his place in the colony. He had contributed nothing. Even his one concrete project—this public garden—was nothing more than a drain on the colony and its artificial ecosystem. And even he had to admit that he was one of the very few who enjoyed the garden. Even if others really did believe it was a good idea, precious few of them made the time to enjoy its beauty, and so Christopher usually found himself alone in this wonderful place.

He sighed again and rubbed his tired eyes. He had not slept well last night. He did, indeed, have a lot of thinking to do. Maybe Mars wasn't the best place for him, after all. The guild would find him a place back on Earth if he requested reassignment. He'd been foolish to think that he could make any difference here. He'd hoped that a brand-new world would have a place for thinkers, that perhaps a new world would not repeat the mistakes of an old and dying Earth. But he had been wrong.

He was just about to go back to his tiny cubicle when he heard the gate open. It was lunchtime, he thought, and perhaps a young couple had decided to come here to escape the prying eyes of the colony. It was one of the few places where people might actually find themselves alone. He stood up and moved away towards the east gate. The least he could do was grant the visitors some privacy.

"Shamin Berry," a voice called, and he turned around, his hand on the gate.

He squinted into the artificial sunlight and saw a man walking towards him. It was Commander Riley.

"Commander," Christopher said, unable to conceal his surprise at seeing Riley here, of all places. It certainly must be trouble, he thought, and wondered what he had done wrong to bring about a personal visit from the commander.

"Shamin Berry. I knew I'd find you here."

"Is... something wrong, Commander?"

"I—we—need your assistance. We've found something extraordinary in the Alba Mons dig."

Christopher laughed.

"You're joking, right? I'm not an archeologist, remember? Or have you forgotten the debriefing speech you gave me?  Please, Commander, I have some serious personal questions I'm pondering right now.  This isn't a good time to ridicule me."

Riley stopped and looked at him with his hard blue eyes.  He dropped his gaze for a moment before he met Christopher's eyes one more time.

"Shamin Berry, I am not the kind of man who has either the time or the energy for practical jokes or ridicule.  As much as it pains me to admit it, the colony has a need for your services.  Now, will you come with me, or should I place an emergency request earthside for the services of another guild philosopher?"

Christopher stared at Riley for a full minute before nodding slowly.

"At your service, Sir," he said meekly.

The Commander led him through the west gate and past the lunchtime crowd at the dining hall.  Occasional heads turned, surprised to see this unlikely duo together.

"Commander, what exactly do you need from me?'

"I'll explain everything in due time, Shamin Berry," he said.

They left the dining hall and entered the corridor leading to the main scientific section of the dome.  Christopher correctly guessed that Riley was taking him to his office.  He could scarcely control his curiosity and excitement.  For the first time the commander was treating him with respect.  What could possibly have happened that would call for his services?

They entered the commander's office and Riley motioned for him to sit down.

"Shamin Berry, first I must advise you that what I am about to tell you has the highest security clearance and must be treated with the utmost confidentiality."

Christorpher nodded.   "I have a level three clearance," he said.

"Good.  Then I will have no reason to worry."

The commander paced across his office and back again before sitting down, not at his desk but in a chair across from Christopher.

"Early this morning the excavation crews discovered a new Martian artifact, unlike anything we've ever seen before," he said, looking deep into Christopher's eyes. "This artifact seems to be some sort of robot left behind by the Martians and buried for almost 3 million years. During the process of excavating the object, it was activated."

"What has this got to do with philosophy?" Christopher asked.

Riley smiled. "You're not going to believe this," he said. "But the robot wants to know about philosophy."

Christopher laughed. "You are kidding, right?"

"I'm afraid I'm not. And to complicate the matter, the robot is programmed to self-destruct—unless we can convince it that we're civilized enough to be worthy of the ancient Martian knowledge. And if it does self-destruct it's liable to take the entire colony with it."

"So you want me to teach this robot about human philosophy?"

"Precisely. And you have just three standard hours to do it."

"And if I can't convince the robot that we're civilized?"

"We've left enough time to return it to where its destruction won't harm the colony—we think. But the loss of scientific knowledge would be irreplaceable."

"All right," Christopher said. "I guess it's about time I carried my own weight around here."

Riley nodded curtly.

"What can you tell me about this robot?"

Riley stood up and paced across the office again. "Well, it doesn't look like much. In fact, the excavation crew thought it was a piece of art when they first dug it up. It's just half a meter high and weighs just 5 kilos. It's pyramid-shaped, made from silicon, has light sensors, and transmits digital code on microwave frequencies. We've unraveled the code—or, actually, the 'bot has unraveled it for us so we can understand it through an interface unit in the main computer. It isn't much to look at, but the thing seems to have the entire wisdom of the Martian culture stored inside its memory."

"And it will only give this knowledge out to another civilization?"

"That's right. And only one it deems worthy."

"But why a philosopher?"

Ruiley shrugged. "We hooked our mainframe to it in an attempt to share knowledge, but it stopped us and wanted to know about philosophy. The computer isn't equipped to handle such things. It fed in the raw data, but the 'bot couldn't understand. That's where you come it."

"So I have three hours to make an alien contraption understand a few thousand years of human thought?"

"That's right. So, we'd best be going. The 'bot is waiting for you in the main lab."

Christopher swallowed hard and wondered how a robot programmed by an alien race would understand concepts that he, a registered philosopher, was still wrestling with.

The commander was right about one thing—the robot wasn't much to look at. It looked like a milky glass pyramid that had been left in the sand for too long. It was hard to imagine that this object was older than the human race.

The robot had been placed on a metal cart. Every now and then a reddish glow would blink from somewhere deep inside the object. Several technicians and scientists lingered around, apparently waiting for him to arrive. Christopher looked at Riley.

"Please sit down," Riley said. "You may speak to it directly."

Christopher sat on a lab stool and looked at the robot for a moment. He had never felt so awkward in his life, not even when Riley had been calling him a parasite.

"I just... talk to it?"

Riley nodded.

"Umm... I am Shamin Christopher Berry, a registered philosopher with the Federated Philosophers Guild. You've asked us to explain human philosophy?"

The red light inside the 'bot illuminated for a moment. Then a female voice came through the speakers of the computer.

"Affirmative."

"Do you... do you have a name?"

"Question mark."

"It doesn't understand," Riley said.

"Ah... what shall I call you?" Christopher asked.

The red light flickered again. "You may call me Robbie."

"The robot from 'Forbidden Planet.' Do I detect a robot with a sense of humor?"

The red light flickered again, longer this time.

"You are correct that I took the name from your database on 20$^{th}$ century films, which your computer shared with me. But I do not understand the term 'humor.' Your database offers no adequate definition of that term."

"Humor is a difficult concept to define."

"Many of your concepts are difficult to define," the robot said. "The database tells me nothing about them. When I seek to learn about humor, I see images of members of your species injuring themselves and each other. I do not understand this term."

"Have you examined the databases of our philosophers?" Christopher asked.

"I have examined them and while I see the words and the images, I do not understand the concepts. So many terms are so poorly defined."

"What is your overall impression of humanity?"

The red flight flickered on and off several times, as if the robot were in deep thought.

"Overall, I am not impressed. Your species has a long history of destruction. You have destroyed yourselves, each other, and are even now destroying your planet. My creators were builders, not destroyers. I believe our ideas are incompatible."

"Yet you will destroy yourself."

"As I have been programmed to do to prevent my knowledge from falling into the wrong hands. Where it can be used for further destruction."

Christopher took a deep breath and looked around the room. He felt the eyes of the entire colony—of the entire human race—upon him.

"My race are builders, too," he said. "We are creators."

"Yet I see destruction in your database," the robot replied.

"Don't you see the words of the great philosophers—of Shakespeare and Milton, and Plato?"

The light flickered for what seemed like a very long time.

"I see the words. But I do not understand. The words do not all define."

"Like humor?"

"Like humor," the robot agreed.

"Then perhaps I should show you something that my people have built," Christopher said.

"I have seen your dome and your city and your spacecraft," the robot said. "They are creations, but they are created in order to conquer and destroy."

"No," Christopher said. "I will show you something else we have built. Something that was built just for the sake of creation."

The light flickered.

"This I would see," the robot said.

Christopher motioned for Riley.

"Have your men bring it to the garden," he said.

Riley frowned. "We don't have much time."

"I know. I'm just hoping that this thing can see. I mean, really see."

The procession was a strange one at best, with two technicians carefully wheeling a silicon pyramid through the corridors of the domed city, flanked by a commander with a degree in astrophysics, and a registered guild philosopher. Christopher was silent, wondering how he could make a glorified silicon chip understand obtuse concepts such as humor or love. Beauty, perhaps. That was his only hope. If only the thing could see and comprehend beauty—yet that was something his own people didn't seem to understand.

Christopher entered the garden first and he directed the technicians to bring "Robbie" over to the bench, which offered the best view of the garden. The robot's red light flickered and flashed erratically while one of the technicians hooked up a portable computer to translate.

"All right," Christopher said. "Can you see your surroundings?"

"I can sense patterns of light and darkness," the robot said.

"And color? Can you sense color?"

"Yes. I can distinguish light waves from what you would term the visible spectrum."

"Good. Then I would like you to take some time to study the visible spectrum around you. This is a place that my people constructed."

The light flickered on and off in a regular pattern for several minutes.

"What is the purpose of this place?" the robot asked.

"Before I answer, are you familiar with our definitions of smell and sound?"

"Yes. I can recreate these sensations within my circuits."

"Good. Then I would like to you recreate these sensations, along with that of sight, and experience this place for several moments."

"Affirmative," the robot said, and its red light changed to a light blue, which flickered on and off in a regular pattern.

After several minutes, the robot spoke.

"I have experienced these sensations. Now tell me, why was this place created?"

"It was created to be beautiful," Christopher said. "And nothing more."

The robot seemed to ponder the matter.

"Does it serve a useful purpose? Are the life forms edible?"

"It does produce a small amount of oxygen, but that isn't why we built it. The water that it requires far offsets the benefits of the oxygen."

"This is a place of beauty?"

"Yes. My people come here just to experience the colors, the smells, and the quiet sounds."

The robot was silent for another full minute and its blue light returned.

"I now understand the term 'beauty'. It is a concept my creators knew well. It is a philosophy that our civilizations share."

"Then you will share knowledge of your creators with us?" Commander Riley asked.

The red light returned and flickered.

"Slowly and over time," the robot said. "I am afraid that the contents of my database would be as incomprehensible to you as the term 'humor' is to me. But in time, we will learn. We will begin with this idea of beauty. It is a common language between us."

That is a good start," Christopher said.

The robot's light turned blue again. "Now," it said, "allow me to remain here and experience more of this thing called 'beauty.' Then, when my sensors are satisfied, we can communicate again."

The robot hummed slowly as its blue light pulsated.

Christopher smiled. This had been a good day, he thought.

# Our Last Ice Giant Exploration
Lauren McBride

After your comm went silent,
I found you - faceplate broken,
air all but gone, unresponsive.

I dragged you back up the steep
sides of the icy crevasse, my
envirosuit's claw-toed boots
supporting us both, praying for
strength, avoiding the shattered
ledge where you fell, pulling you
across the frozen plain to our
heated dome home, willing
you back to consciousness.

Your heart never stopped beating,
but I think I am no longer
treasured there from the way
you never say my name,
the way you never say
anything at all.

# A Cloud on Fire
## Jason Lairamore

A mauve-colored Sun cast sickly purple hues onto the world below, where jagged, scarlet mountaintops crashed upon each other like cresting waves frozen in time. Those mountain peaks seemed to claw at the ill-colored sky.

Beneath the peaks lay rocky mountainsides that descended roughly into the deeper haze that hid the true surface of the strange planetoid.

Tervel Lampkin kept close to the dangerous-looking rock formations so that his camera might give a good accounting of this angry-looking place. The Worm Sport audience back home, who were many light years away, expected only the best.

His focus was on the great gray cloud billowing out from between the two mountain ranges. A rolling blue flame wafted thickly about the gray cloud. Even given the multitude of vast and strange places he had seen on previous wormhole rift jumps, he had yet to see anything like that. Even the sensitive ship gear was at a loss to discern the exact cause of the odd visual effect.

With a push of a button, he stopped his ship and swiveled his piloting chair around so that he could start the ship's internal camera rolling.

The view could not have been better. There he sat, wearing his asparagus-green turtleneck that had a large, gold '1' on its chest. His eyes, which were cerulean blue, stared wide and seeking toward the camera and the watching audience. Fine lines creased his mahogany tanned skin as he smiled at the worlds back home. He turned his head slightly to the right to draw attention to the spectacular view behind him of the baby-blue flames surrounding the gray cloud.

"Tervel Lampkin here, your favorite Rifter, and, as you can see, I've discovered something quite wonderful." He widened his eyes a trifle. "The sensors don't know what to make of it."

He couldn't help but think that he might have hit the jackpot this time.

He stood from his chair and struck a wide-legged, challenging pose.

"Keep watching, as I explore something never seen before."

The ship's internal camera clicked over to his uni transport as he walked the short distance to the little flyer. In short order, he was inside its single seat and strapped in. He gave the camera a salute as he closed the clear shell over himself.

Moments later, the little uni dropped from the belly of the main ship and started making its way toward the mass of blue flames. He kept a close eye on his external sensory gear as he neared. He knew from past experience that he would have to be fast if something unexpected happened.

Clenching his jaw, he advanced into the blue flames. To pause, to show any kind of hesitation, would play out badly for those watching back home. He had seen the negative effects of displayed doubt a few times against some of his fellow Rifters. None of them had ever recovered their standings afterward, no matter what new and amazing thing they did.

The masses were a fickle beast to please.

The temperature on the shell of his uni shot up to over 3,000 degrees Centigrade and he almost hit the return boosters before realizing that the temperature had leveled off. He shook his head and grinned at the little dash camera. His scalp itched as beads of sweat formed under his spiky, blond hair, but he resisted the urge to scratch it.

"A little warmer than I expected," he said to the viewing audience, and he wasn't joking. The computers had told him that the blue flame should have topped out at around 1300 Centigrade.

It was but another nugget of data for the scientists to puzzle over.

The uni was working hard to maintain its internal temperature, and it was failing, but he couldn't stop now.

He hit the display button on his dashboard so that the people back home could see the steadily rising temperature. 30, 32, the numbers kept climbing.

The gray cloud was getting closer. He pushed the dual display so that the camera showed both him and the nearing mass of dense, gray fog. Still, his sensors were coming up blank on the make-up of whatever constituted the rolling mass.

"I hope it's a little cooler in there," he said.

He raised his eyebrows as he focused his attention to all the eyes he knew were watching him. He had just started to smile at his own little jest when the gray cloud boiled out and engulfed his little ship.

Instinctively, he hit the return button. The world went dark. The little uni trembled like a scared puppy then cracked. The front of the ship and the panel before him crunched as if under tremendous pressure. He sucked in a breath and pushed against the clear, vibrating shielding above his head.

The last thing he thought before everything exploded into star bursts behind his eyes was that the gray cloud had seemed to sense him and attack.

\* \* \*

He blinked to awareness inside the shiny, metal recovery tube aboard his ship. He shook his head and focused on the little mirror directly in front of his face.

"I am never wrong," he told his reflection.

Besides the mirror was a display showing the last moment of the uni's flight before it was crunched into a can of sardines. He couldn't believe that enough of him had lived to allow for regeneration.

"Be-lop, Betty, I owe you two a beer," he said from within the cylindrical tube holding his body. He could feel a number of wires and needles poking from his skin as well as more than a few nutrition and drug patches.

"You owe them more than that, Lamp," a voice called over the tube's communication system.

His blood ran cold when he heard that voice. Only one person in all the worlds called him 'Lamp', and she should not be here. Nobody should. But here she was.

Regen Barl, the one and only, was inside his ship. Regen, the Mars-born Rifter who had taken the game to new heights with her discovery of alien ruins, and the only person with more points than him in the game, had been sent here, to his logged discovery.

"Pop the top on this can, Betty," he said.

The recovery tube rotated to a standing position and beeped in warning before the needles and wires retracted from his body. He tried not to wince at the pain it caused as the tube hissed open, coffin style.

"Come to see me rise from the dead?" he asked as he stepped out and onto the ship's metal floor. Betty, the designated doctor robot, handed him a robe to cover his nakedness. He took the robe and tried not to shake as he donned the garment, but, man-alive, did he feel weak. He glanced at Be-lop, the defense bot, and gave him a salute.

"Thanks for saving me from the trash compactor, Be-lop."

"You were three weeks in the can," Regen said. He jerked in surprise and frowned up at her. She was a tall woman, beautiful and thin, with black hair and very white skin. A row of freckles lined her high cheekbones and nose.

"Longest recovery to date," she continued and smiled. "Broke the record." Her lips were thin, but they seemed to match the long angles of her face in a way that made her even more attractive.

"Try to keep up if you can," he said. Internally, he was calculating the distance this hunk of rock had traveled from his point of entry in three weeks. He would have to leave soon, or he would be too far away to make the trip back to his wormhole.

Regen folded her long arms across her thin chest and smiled again, showing more teeth this time. She wore a red spandex one-piece. The color worked well for her.

"I don't know if I'll be able to top this," she said. "It looks like you guessed right on this wormhole."

"I'm never wrong," he muttered as he walked on trembling legs to the built-in armoire where he kept his clothes.

"That's what you keep saying," she said.

"Why are you here, Regen?" he asked as he stepped into a black under-suit. He continued to dress in some tan cargo pants and another of his asparagus turtlenecks with the embossed golden '1'.

"The gaming commission thinks you might have hit the jackpot," she said.

Since the beginning of Worm Sport some fifteen years ago, the grand prize, the only prize that really, truly mattered, had been the discovery of living alien intelligence, and, to date, only Regen had found anything remotely close.

"Why are *you* here?" he asked again. This planetoid was his discovery, his fame. The commission hadn't called on him to assist Regen when she had found the now-infamous destroyed alien outpost on that hunk of broken rock she had investigated more than a year ago.

Regen tightened her eyes at him for a heartbeat, studying him. She always pouted when she was thinking. Her lips would push out a little in an almost kissing gesture.

"You won't believe it coming from me. Check your glasses."

He was tempted to kick her off his ship right then and there just to establish a firmer hand in the proceedings, but he didn't. When it came right down to it, he respected Regen too much to stoop to petty measures. She would see through such an act, anyway. She hadn't gotten to be a Rifter because of her pretty face.

His glasses were where he had left them before the little uni trip that had almost killed him. He walked to the bridge of his ship and unplugged them from the consol. Regen followed.

The glasses had clear lenses and were horn rimmed. He turned to look at her and she did a little curtsy as the computer in the glasses pinged her. All her public data bubbled beside her in lettering that contrasted to the background of the ship's walls.

She was still number one on the Worm Sport record boards. His score hadn't changed. That shouldn't be. The records were always updated to account for the wormhole jump risk. He flipped to his record and found that the end location of his jump hadn't even been filed.

"They have you listed as MIA," Regen said, anticipating that he had checked that first. There was a message blinking in the top right of his vision. He focused on the red, flashing dot and a video file opened.

Commissioner Jeron Fontil sat on the edge of his desk in his private office located in the Commission's office building on the Earth's moon. He was old enough to garner the respect granted to the older generation, but young enough that his vitality still showed. He wore a suit, the antiquated style with a white shirt and colorful tie, and had just enough of a paunch that he looked only mildly out of peak shape.

"Straight to it, Mr. Lampkin," the Commissioner said. He had put away his usual patient nature that Tervel had seen any number of times on the news vids. "You may have stumbled onto something. The government knows and is watching. Your ship feed will be restricted until confirmation, but keep on acting like everyone is watching so that we won't have to edit too much when the time comes to air your find. Regen Barl delivered the modified tech you two will need to get into the cloud.

"I know time is short. You'll have to make this investigation quick if you hope to make it back to the wormhole. So go, and give us a good show."

The Commissioner made a motion to cut the feed, but stopped the action halfway through.

"And don't worry," he said with a casual smile. "All the points for this expedition will go to your score."

The video file ended.

Regen was looking out the port windows from the bridge. He took his glasses off and plugged them back into the ship's control panel.

"I hope you found it," she said, her back to him. From the tone of her voice she sounded sincere. A memory of how the cloud had shot out and surrounded his uni replayed in his mind.

"I think I did," he said.

She turned to look at him, her pale face set and intense.

"How can you be so sure?"

He stared back at her and matched her seriousness.

"I am never wrong."

She shook her head and rolled her eyes, then turned to look back out at the gray cloud surrounded by blue flames.

\* \* \*

They walked the short distance between their joined ships and entered her spaceship.

The two-seater was quite a sight. Curvy and gold plated, it looked like something straight off the cover of Worm Sport Technologies Magazine. More than likely, if this little venture paid the dividends that Tervel expected, the ship might very well end up on said cover.

He whistled his appreciation as he ran a finger down the flier's sexy side panel.

"Don't make me jealous," Regen said jokingly from her position in front of the computer board against one of the ship's walls.

"There's no comparison," he said, still eyeing the machine. There were more dials and displays on the dash than he was used to, but a quick glance told him that he would be able to read them without a problem. Danger levels were always marked in red. As long as he hit the return booster when the dial was in that section, he should be able to stay alive.

"I hope this little minx gets us through the cloud," she said, turning from her computer work. "As for what lies beyond that," she shrugged.

He climbed into the driver's seat.

"I'm ready if you are," he said.

She didn't object to him driving, and he was glad. This was still his wormhole find, after all.

They dropped from the main ship after she took her seat and strapped in. The blue flames were a rolling mass that filled their vision.

"Not that I'm complaining," she said after a few moments, "but, of all the Rifters, why did they choose me to follow you down this particular hole?"

The answer to that question was obvious to Tervel.

"Your face has already been stamped on the search for aliens," he said. "After this, my pretty mug will be etched right there next to yours."

They entered the flames without a hitch. The temperature rose as it had before, but this rig was geared to handle it and much more besides.

The gray fog boiled out as it had before and engulfed them.

The ship beeped and Tervel tensed. He scanned the dials and the front of the ship for signs of the terrible pressure that had so nearly cost him his life just a few short weeks ago. His finger hovered over the return booster button.

An undulation in the metal on the front of the ship almost sent his finger down upon that button, but he held the reflex in check. The metal bent, but did not break. He frowned as he leaned forward to study it closer. The ship's metal undulated like a wave, dipping and rising in a strange rhythm. Soon, the entire external portion of the ship, including the clear covering overhead, was doing the same.

"Must be sonic," Regen said. Tervel didn't even spare her a comment. His attention was focused on the ship around him, looking for the first sign of possible hull failure.

"We look like a worm inching along," she continued.

Her assessment couldn't have been more spot-on. Whatever force the gray cloud exerted was being shifted smoothly by the dynamic action of the ship's hull.

They were digging their way deeper into the cloud.

It took fifteen minutes to make it through. The flier's nose exited first and hung over an abyss of pure black.

"That's a different medium," Regen said.

Tervel hadn't paid any great attention to the console sensor readouts. He focused on the blackness in front of them and tried to discern if anything was in the gloom.

The remainder of the ship followed the front. They were free of the dense, gray cloud, but instead of falling, as Tervel had assumed would happen, the ship floated, almost as if it was being buoyed. The flier even rocked, just like a ship at sea.

"It's gel-like," Regen said. "We're sinking deeper into it."

Tervel nodded and looked over his shoulder. He could not see the gray cloud, or anything for that matter. There was only blackness.

He raised his eyebrows and turned to look at Regen.

"We're past the point of no return," he said. "There is no way the bots can come get us if we run into trouble. They might make it for a short time in the cloud, but they would be pulverized before reaching anywhere near where we are."

Regen sighed as she gazed into the blackness.

The two-seater dropped free of the black gel in an instant and the altitude jets came online. They hovered just below a pool of inky black. Under them, and all around, was a diffuse, brown luminescence. Such was the light that Tervel could only see about ten meters in any direction.

"Sensors show rocky ground seventy meters below us," Regen said.

"Let's go," he said.

"The sensors are having trouble being effective past a hundred meters," she continued as he drove the ship straight down. "Something about the environment is muting long range sensors. We won't be getting a map."

"So we explore."

"Lamp?"

"Regen."

"What will we do if we find aliens?"

He shrugged as he continued to scan the limited visibility surrounding the ship. She was asking, he knew, not because she would defer to his judgment on whatever unknown situation they might find themselves in, but because she wanted to make sure they acted together if the need arose.

He looked at her and shook his head.

"If we find intelligent life, everything changes, no matter what we do."

The ship landed with a soft thud.

\* \* \*

The atmosphere outside wasn't exactly breathable, but it wouldn't kill them right off either. A thin protective suit to cover their skin would be enough to keep them alive. They might be a little warm, but that was a small price to pay. At least it meant they could leave the ship without donning a full space suit. Those things, though wonderful, were clunky.

Regen was the first to set foot on the surface, and he didn't begrudge her. They had both been to a great many hunks of rock. The novelty of walking on a strange surface had lost its collective awe. It was what the place looked like, how it felt, and anything out of the ordinary that continued to hold sway for those viewing back home.

"So far, nothing," Regen said. She had taken a few steps away from the flier while he stuffed a couple packs full of every possible thing they might need. He handed her one, and after she had put it across her shoulders, he handed her a laser pistol.

She paused for the briefest of seconds before accepting the gun. He turned to gaze at the murky brown light.

"Any direction feeling better to you?" he asked.

She shrugged, so he started walking in the direction they were facing. Regen kept her eyes on the sensory outputs detailed on her wrist computer and he kept his eyes on the brown mist for any signs of trouble.

After about a hundred meters of trudging on the broken ground, Regen stopped and slowly turned in a full circle.

"Sensor distortion seems to be coming from that direction," she said. She looked off to their right, as did he, but there was nothing except more of the brown light.

"Lead on," he said.

Regen slowed her already timid pace after another hundred meters.

"It's centralizing," she said.

They were reaching one of the walls of the cavern. He could feel it in the way the air moved and the way sound bounced around from the scuffing of their boots.

Twenty steps later he saw it. A massive half circle of the black, gel-like substance lay against the cavern's wall. He raised his gun and pointed it at the inky smoothness. Regen touched his extended arm lightly and he almost pulled the trigger.

"Let's go get the flier and see if we can fly through," she said.

He took a deep breath and nodded just as a piercing greenish-yellow light blazed down from a position above the black gel. He raised his arm and shot at the blinding light. He couldn't believe that he hit the light source, but the brightness blinked off as suddenly as it had come.

"Drop your weapon," a voice boomed.

"English?" Regen said in a hushed whisper.

Tervel didn't care at the moment.

"No," he called back.

A pause followed. The eerie quiet of the cavern gave him time to consider just how precarious their situation was. Sure, it had been that way from the start, but now that actual contact had been made, reality seemed to settle more firmly into his bones.

"We are Rifters," Regen said under her breath.

Yeah, she was feeling it too.

The black gel in front of them rolled like someone had come along and dropped a pebble on its surface. This time, when he raised his gun, Regen raised hers too.

An archway formed in the blackness, revealing a walkway wide enough for both of them to travel side by side. At the tunnel's far end, a green-tinted light spilled out. He kept his gun pointed at the tunnel, but Regen dropped hers to her side.

"Lower your laser, Lamp," she said. "We aren't here to fight, and besides, they have the home field advantage."

She was right, of course. He lowered his gun as a large creature padded on four short legs toward them. He almost raised his gun again, but held back.

When the creature was on their side of the black gel it stopped and stood on its hind legs. It achieved this by first bending its back like a hinge joint in its middle then whipping upright by shifting its center of gravity.

It looked like a lizard, complete with a tail, green and white scales, a prominent mouth, and holes in the side of its head instead of ears. Aside from its size, the differences between a true Earth lizard and this creature were its arms and its eyes. The arms were long, and had an extra set of elbows. Its hands had six digits, two of which appeared to be thumbs. Its feet had a set of vicious-looking claws that dug into the gravelly floor.

The eyes were more different still. They were a uniform gray, large, upwardly angled, and ovoid in shape.

When it spoke, its voice came from a metal box lying on a chain around its long neck. The noise that issued forth sounded like a string of snake hisses and frog croaks.

The creature glanced down at the box on its chest and back at them.

"My name and home world did not translate. I am sorry."

Tervel glanced at the box and then at the creature.

"How is it that you understand English?" he asked.

The creature's tongue licked out a full foot from its protruding mouth before it answered.

"We became aware of you the moment you first came into contact with the ward shield and have been studying you and your ship ever since to prepare for your arrival."

Regen spoke. "If you knew we were outside, why not introduce yourselves?"

"We were not prepared," it said.

Tervel shook his head. That may have been an answer, but it wasn't the whole answer.

"Are there other intelligent species out there?" he asked. He knew that by asking the creature the question he was potentially revealing their ignorance on the matter, but he felt the possible risk necessary. They were ignorant, after all.

The lizard tasted the air again with its long, forked tongue. The action was disconcerting. It made him feel like the alien was sniffing him as a human would a steak fresh from the grill.

"You are the first sentient species we have encountered," it said.

"This isn't your home world," Regen said. The creature focused its flat, expressionless eyes on her and flicked its tongue out again. Tervel felt the impulse to step in front of her, to protect her, but held himself in check.

"We are traveling to another star system," the thing said, "to another planet so that we might expand our race."

"We found ruins of an alien race on the surface of an asteroid," Regen said.

Tervel frowned and glanced over at her.

"That was one of our earlier attempts to leave our home system," the alien followed. "Surface travel was abandoned. Radiation and errant space debris make it impossible."

Regen smiled from ear to ear and Tervel couldn't blame her. Here was one of the alien beings whose people had built the crumbled structure she had originally discovered.

"How is it that you found us?" the creature asked.

"Artificial wormholes," Regen said immediately.

The lizard stared at her.

"I do not understand," it said.

"Technology," Tervel supplied.

"We could learn so much from each other," Regen said.

The creature's tongue shot out again as it considered her words.

"You are welcome to join us," it said.

Tervel shook his head. That wasn't going to happen. Truly, they were pushing the limits of their time on this planetoid as it was. Every moment spent here carried them farther and farther away from the wormhole he had entered a few weeks ago.

He opened his mouth to say as much when Regen piped in.

"I'd like that."

"No," he said, forcefully.

She turned and looked at him like he was the alien.

"We can leave monitoring equipment. We can keep track of where it is they are going," he said.

They didn't even know how long of a trip this hunk of rock would have to make before it reached its destination. For all they knew, this installation was set up as a generation ship. He couldn't believe she was willing to commit the rest of her life with beings that she had just met.

She studied him a moment longer then seemed to come to a decision. He could tell by the set of her jaw and the hardness of her eyes.

All he saw on her face was disappointment.

He shook his head, his ire rising at the unspoken judgment he felt coming from her.

"I'm never wrong," he said. Surely she saw the folly of blindly jumping into an unknown situation.

She just shook her head.

\* \* \*

A bad taste filled his mouth during the flier trip back to his ship. Once on board, he remotely set Regen's spaceship to seek out a safe landing spot on the murky, purple surface below, then headed for the wormhole that would take him home. He performed all the necessary tasks quickly and quietly. His eagerness to be away consumed him, and the bitterness of leaving Regen behind angered him. He could not for the life of him understand why she had left everything she had known behind.

After he had reached space and locked in the coordinates, he entered the sleep tube. It would take him a couple weeks of hard spaceflight to reach the hole, and he didn't want to spend that time aching over the way he and Regen had parted. She had made her decision and that was that. Maybe the induced sleep would help clear his head.

But upon waking a short distance from the wormhole, he found that nothing had changed. From his piloting chair, he pulled up the show of him and Regen that had gone out for all the worlds to see.

The gaming commission had done very little editing of their trip into the blue flames and the gray cloud. He watched it to the very end, where he had silently turned his back on Regen and walked away. The camera view stayed with his retreating back for a few steps then shifted to a close-up of Regen's beautiful face.

"I am a Rifter," she said quietly, before the screen went black.

He stared into the silent, blank screen as the realization of his mistake settled heavily on his chest. He'd run away while she had stayed. She'd taken the ultimate leap into the unknown and the worlds back home would love it like no other. She had done exactly what a Rifter was supposed to do.

He had hesitated. He had doubted. No. It couldn't be.

He had been wrong.

His ship entered the wormhole and he was back in known space in the blink of an eye.

# Watch Where You Step!
## Lauren McBride

All of us down here
delighted to learn

of the upcoming peace treaty
with you giant, aggressive,

big-footed Terrans wontonly
invading our world

after finally making you
understand that we Martians

are not merely tiny microbes
teeming underground.

# The Gray Area
## Travis Lee

The pod opened and Griff took his first breath in over 400 years.

He gasped for air, warmth spreading through his body as the long sleep ended and he could feel and move once more. He tried his fingers first, slowly curling them into a fist. Then he bent his elbows and waited for his legs.

Griff's feet reached the end of the pod and he watched them, stiff, white, consequence of the long sleep. Explorers enjoyed dreams during the long sleep but Griff could remember nothing. No dreams, no thoughts. Only a vast emptiness between Earth and here, between then and now.

400 years. The pod was silver inside, no bed. Tendrils below him unplugged from his back, pinprick wounds leaking no blood. When he first woke, he stared through the plexiglass hatch of the pod at a kaleidoscope of colors in an alien sky his earthborne eyes could make little sense of, not fearing the long days of labor awaiting him but resigned to his fate, the readout to his left giving the current year on Earth.

Griff's feet warmed up. He wiggled his toes and then he gazed up at the kaleidoscope of colors. Too many to catalog. The light on this planet bending in twilight or sunrise, he couldn't tell, and he leaned up, gripping the sides of the pod.

He turned his head from side to side, taking measure of his surroundings. A vast alien forest, no Master Droid to wake him. Colonization was challenging, and it attracted either the daring or the desperate.

Griff slung a leg over the side of the pod, certain the Master Droid would come skulking along to dart an obedience chip into the base of his neck. Griff listened. Caw of an alien bird looped in his ears and fell silent. Flowery aroma in the air. No shipboard announcements. No calls to duty.

Griff slung his other leg over and fell. He went rolling downhill, slamming to a stop at the base of a thick tree. He panted, and after he'd caught his breath, he lay on his back, looking up. The tree's branches were knotted like roots.

The same kaleidoscope light shimmered on the leaves.

The leaves were the size and shape of turtle shells. Griff took deep, deliberate breaths, steadying himself. He wore the bright orange uniform of a convict. Men to be sold for free labor, lay the foundations for a new civilization and die. The day the Master Droid sealed Griff in the pod for his long sleep he'd gone willingly. Others fought. But fight or no fight, you would not escape. Griff had gone under knowing that a short and brutal life awaited him on the new planet.

He stood, balancing himself on the tree. The pod glistened with the polish of proud Martian engineering, no kaleidoscope of colors claiming it, and Griff hunkered down on the other side of the tree, aware that something had gone terribly wrong.

\* \* \*

Griff staggered through the forest. The insects and birds on this planet sounded similar to those on Earth and Griff focused on their chirping, drifting away from his orange uniform to his boyhood in Astor. Slum boys learned quick and their lessons were harsh, none harsher than those in Sue Boy. Shacks atop shacks atop shacks, homes built from the detritus of the great wars, radiation levels safe enough for life to blossom once more. The drug lord breathed his own air supply, his lungs so twisted from years of smoking the silver spider, and a young Griff had gaped at the twin cannisters feeding the drug lord's gas mask, keeping him from suffocating in the same air passing through billions of lungs each day.

A trickle of water stirred Griff from this reverie. The long sleep had robbed him of everyone he'd ever known and Griff forced himself to concentrate on the noise, following it beneath the turtle shell leaves and their kaleidoscope colors. The air was still. The water trickled and Griff passed between the trees and came upon the pond.

A thin creek fed it. The water as still as the air and in it the colors bent in an ongoing geometry of shapes too familiar for comfort. In the middle of the pond bloomed a flower as tall and as thick as any tree here, open at the top, its petals lolling loose, pink and bloated like swollen tongues.

Griff reached for the water and stopped himself, making fists and driving them into his thighs. This planet was safe to inhabit—that much was certain. The air was breathable, but the water?

*It drew you here. It will lure others too.*

If they were close by. Griff had no notion of how large this planet was or how far the other pods were. Caught up in panic, fearing the arrival of the Master Droid, Griff fled into the woods and laid flat on his stomach, gazing at the pond through the grass.

A spit of gray blighted the closest grass blade and Griff looked past it, at the pond and the flower. He thought about the ship. It likely crashed, but not before launching the pods. Sabotage? Malfunction? He had no way of knowing. Colonists died often, that's why it attracted the daring or the desperate, and the spread of the pods would depend on how high in orbit the ship was when it ejected them. The pods had their own nav system for safe landings, but surely some had died, colonists, slaves.

Crew?

Griff narrowed his eyes on the grass blade, the gray contaminating it. No kaleidoscope here. He checked the other grass blades—they too contained their own dashes of gray. Griff pinched the tip of a grass blade, studying it for a moment, then he crawled backwards, got to his feet, and left the pond.

\* \* \*

The alien forest neither thinned nor thickened and Griff staggered through it, his stomach aching, his mouth dry. He spotted a creature similar in shape to a rabbit hopping through the grass. Two spiral horns protruded from its head like the tips of a stabbing fork. Its eyes glittered with the kaleidoscope pattern and Griff dove at it, his fingers hooked like killing claws, and seized only grass.

Griff smelled smoke, and he dropped to his stomach. He crawled, gently pushing fallen branches out of his way. He'd started out as an ear boy for the drug lord. In Sue Boy the drug lord's word was law and it was young Griff's duty to sneak around the slums, crawling through the tiniest spaces, recording the whispers of treason and reporting back so the schemers could face slum justice.

That Griff had been small, malnourished. This Griff's stomach groaned and he paused to let it pass. The sky was cloudless in this world's night, the kaleidoscope of colors fading in the heavens. A fire raged, an intruder, and peeking over his forearm, Griff took measure of them.

They wore the silver uniforms of the ship's crew, hard to tell their ranks in the dim firelight. One of them had his arm in a sling and they sat in the grass, containers behind them, no doubt thumbprint or retina locked. Griff thought there might be six in the contingent, maybe more.

His gaze drifted from the fire consuming the alien wood to the containers. He counted at least three, and his stomach groaned. Youth struggling in the Sue Boy slums, sustenance their payment. Soon young Griff would earn more than food and he could still remember his first payment, a single slice of bread. Plain, but young Griff had wolfed it down, taking care to lick the crumbs off his palms and his stomach growled, his eyes not leaving the containers until the man with his arm in the sling broke from the group and trotted his way.

\* \* \*

Griff crawled backward, his heart racing, grabbing the nearest tree like a drowning man clinging to a life preserver. He rolled to the other side of the tree and tried to calm his breathing.

The heavy fall of boots drew closer. They stopped and Griff closed his eyes, he swallowed.

His stomach growled.

Griff scrambled to his feet and snatched the man and shoved him to the ground, hand on his mouth, fingers poised at his windpipe.

"Not a word," Griff whispered. "Or I'll tear your windpipe."

The man struggled, and Griff pinched his windpipe.

"Stop," Griff whispered.

The man went still. Griff said, "I'm removing my hand. You make a noise, you die. Understand?"

The man nodded. Griff removed his hand from the man's mouth and patted his uniform, down his ribs to his waist, and he withdrew the man's weapon. It was shaped like a gun, but the readout at the base told a different story: a stunner.

"You don't have a real gun?" Griff whispered.

"I don't," the man whispered back.

"How about your companions?"

"They don't either."

"Sure." Griff glanced at the fire. "How many?"

"Four."

Griff tightened his grip on the man's windpipe. "Try again."

Griff released him, and the man wheezed, "Nine."

"Regular crew? Security?"

"Three colonists, plus what's left of security."

"What's left..." Griff closed his eyes, his stomach threatening another growl. The hunger and the thirst made it hard to speak, harder still to think. He opened his eyes, the alien world swimming. "What happened?"

"I don't know. Some kind of malfunction, something with the atmosphere. The ship crashed, we abandoned it."

Griff swallowed. "How many survived?"

"We're the only life transport that got out in time, but the ship is okay. It's broadcasting and that's where we're headed."

"Well that's not where you and I are headed. C'mon."

"Wait, wait. I—"

Griff's stomach growled. He closed his eyes until it stopped, the man's next words inducing another growl.

"We got food."

Griff didn't respond.

"Our containers are full of food and the ship's got plenty. We'll share it with you, we don't care that you're a slave. None of that matters now."

Griff's grip on his windpipe relaxed.

"We got lots of food," the man said. He was slowly raising his voice but Griff didn't notice, that single slice of bread had nourished him, reward for a job well done. "Food for days, more than we'll ever need."

The man freed himself from Griff's grip and called out to the others. Griff bashed the man in the temple with the stunner, and his stomach growling, he scrambled to his feet and let loose one stunshot into the commotion around the fire.

Then Griff took off at a dead sprint through the forest.

\* \* \*

Griff tripped and tumbled through the grass, the stunner falling from his hands. He snatched it and rolled over, sweating, clawing for breath. He leveled the stunner at the direction from where he'd fled, the weapon shaking with his hands.

With the shaking weapon aimed, Griff sat up, working his way to his feet. The drug lord had liked him because he was small and fast with a good memory. The drug lord, masked man breathing air that was poison to everyone else but nourishing to him, mechanical voice pouring filtered and scratchy through his gas mask, heaping praise upon young Griff and in the years raising him further in his circle.

Griff's breathing settled, freeing him from the old times. 400 years in the long sleep. Was Sue Boy still standing? Had the ship sent any transmissions back to Earth prior to the crash? Griff thought perhaps, but he couldn't be sure. All he knew was that they were after him now and he backed up a few paces, the trembling stunner focused on the trees ahead of him.

His stomach ached.

His mouth was dry.

Griff turned and shambled through the forest.

When Griff heard the trickle of water, he picked up his pace and fell to his knees at the shore. The ground was inviting, his body yearned to lie down, an urge smothering the cries of his stomach and throat, and Griff took a deep breath. He forced himself to stay up.

The water would attract others. He'd no way to know how they were tracking him, if their radars had survived the crash or if they even worked on this world. Gazing up at the turtle shell leaves and their kaleidoscopes of colors, Griff remarked that this was his fist time seeing a forest in something other than stale images. Alien forest, alien world, breathing alien air and Griff cupped a puddle of alien water in his palm and splashed it in his mouth.

He swished it around his teeth and tongue, ready to spit it out at any foul taste. The water wasn't alien—it was water. He swallowed.

Then he drank more.

He lost all rational thought and heaved handfuls of creekwater in his mouth, drinking until his belly cramped. He keeled over, burped, and set free on a ragged whisper a soft cry of satisfaction.

\* \* \*

The water sloshed around in Griff's stomach as he walked, and he bent over, hands on his knees, letting the nausea pass. He burped. He grasped for the nearest tree and sliding his hand up smooth bark he blinked as the figures stepped into view, one, two, three, all clad in the crew's uniform and clutching rifles.

"Hands," said a bald man with a fierce gaze.

Griff swayed, queasy. A burp rolled toward his throat.

He spun and ran, pushing himself off the tree. The whistle of the stunbolt reached his ears a second before numbness swept over his legs, and he fell on his face, biting into his cheek.

Griff let the blood trickle out his lips. He seized his stunner with both hands and rolled over, training the weapon on the advancing men, and the bald man with the fierce gaze snatched it from him.

"Bind his wrists," the bald man ordered.

\* \* \*

They dragged Griff across the forest by his wrists. They only slowed once: to swap out who was dragging him. Grass, dirt, sticks, Griff stared up at the turtle shell leaves, wincing as a rock nicked his cheek.

They deposited Griff by the fire and then two of them leaned him up on the storage containers. The bald man crouched before Griff, fire blazing behind him and framing him like a feral god. The bald man regarded Griff with cold eyes, a face cut from stone. He wore the uniform of the ship's crew and a sigil of Earth was hooked above his right breast, three blue bars below it.

The bald man waved for the man with his arm in the sling to join them. "This him?"

"Yes sir."

"What's your name?" the bald man asked Griff.

Griff looked around, taking measure of the camp. More people near and behind the fire, maybe six, maybe more. Griff's eyes watered from the heat.

"So," the bald man said, "what's the matter? You can't talk? You threatened Charlie here, put a good scare into him. You know what his job is?"

Griff didn't answer.

"Chronicling. Charlie's name will go into the archives. First Chronicler of Colony 412-3A. Thousands of years from now, schoolchildren will know his name."

Charlie took this without acknowledgement.

"Colony 412-3A," the bald man said. "Now, I don't like that name. After the first generation, it will fall on our descendants to properly christen this place. Or, it would have. See, you're the only survivor. Why is that? Something you planned?"

Griff held down a burp and said, "You're lying."

"Ah, so he does speak. Right, the *Jefferson* dumped the pods prior to crashing. Colonists and slaves alike are scattered all over this planet. Is there anything you need?"

Griff didn't respond. Interrogations were structured the way they were for a reason: they worked. The police rarely entered Sue Boy; bribes and intimidation saw to it. But once you ventured outside the slums, it was a different story. Many people in the drug lord's employ cracked under the lights, no drugs needed, but Griff was made of different stuff. The cops had injected him, but even then only got what the drug lord had deigned to tell him.

The bald man smiled, small, suppressed. His lips were thin and one cheek puffed out, amusement twinkling in his eyes and it was a grotesque expression.

"I see you've played this game before," the bald man said. "No matter. At least let me know your name. We all have names here, crew, colonist..." He gave Griff's uniform a quick glance. "Slave. But, are we all not colonists here on 412-3A? Cooperate, and I could see about getting some better clothes for you. Cooperate—"

*—and I could see about getting you better arrangements. Cooperate, and maybe you won't have to spend the best years of your life behind bars. Cooperate, and—*

"—I'll get you some food. I'll even consider taking those binds off your wrists. No need for binds among equals." The bald man patted Griff on the shoulder and left him alone, Charlie retreating to the other side of the fire.

\* \* \*

They soon dragged Griff to the other side of the fire, where he leaned against a log. Feeling crept back into his legs, but he dared not show it. He kept his legs as limp as he could and assessed his captors.

Griff counted nine, just as Charlie had said, all in the same silver uniform. None of these people were colonists and Griff turned his head, searching for their life transport. He spotted some black lump in the distance, the fire toying with his vision. His eyes watered and he squeezed them shut.

Footsteps drew close and when Griff again opened his eyes, Charlie was on one knee before him.

"Can you move your legs?"

"No."

Charlie scoffed. "Be thankful I'm not Roderick. He'd kick you in the shins to prove you're lying."

"He's the bald man?"

Charlie hummed. "Chain of command defaults to him."

"And what are you?"

Charlie averted his eyes. "Just a junior officer."

"Academy?"

"How'd you know?"

Now it was Griff's turn to scoff. "Maybe I should've gone myself."

"It's not that great."

"Where are the colonists?"

Charlie looked over at the others. Some of them were playing cards on the ground, others were chatting. Two of them, a man and a woman, were racing to see who could reassemble their rifle the fastest. Cheers rose as they neared completion.

Charlie turned back to Griff. "I think you can surmise where the colonists are."

"Not here."

"All the pods launched," Charlie said. "We've no way to track them with the equipment we have, that's back on the *Jefferson*."

"And I'm the first you found."

Griff didn't ask it as a question. In the hierarchy of those serving the drug lord were older boys, men to young Griff, who taught him how to play people. Anyone could be unlocked, all you needed to do was press the right code. Questions posed as statements did their work and young Griff had unveiled a police informant that way, he—

Charlie averted his eyes again. Briefly, but brief was all the confirmation Griff needed.

"Yes," Charlie said. He stood, wincing as his arm shifted in his sling. "We'll get you some food soon."

\* \* \*

Cheers erupted as the woman reassembled her rifle first. The man demanded a rematch, Roderick slinking among them like a panther.

Griff kept an eye on them, thinking of Earth. Sunrise according to his body was not sunrise here, whatever this planet knew as sunrise. The lights in the sky dimmed, they brightened, just enough natural light to make your way and the manmade fire dimmed, chewing through alien logs cut in shapes that were oddly neat and even. Griff thought Charlie might have made it, lowest ranking guy stuck with the most tedious task. When Griff was a teenager he'd visited a military recruitment center, two columns outside displaying the military's exploits in three dimensions. *See the Stars! Explore the Galaxy! Go Down in History*, and below this was a code to scan with your phone: an invitation to step into the metaverse and get a taste firsthand.

Griff hadn't needed the ads or the metaverse; he was hungry, he was desperate. The drug lord by then was dead, rivals not slitting his throat as they had his lieutenants but simply tearing off his gas mask, and letting the very air that nourished twenty billion other people suffocate him.

Was there another informant? Griff thought then as he thought now that you could never be free of informants, no matter how brutal the repercussions. The police had their own ways of ensnaring people, and so did the military—Griff knew others from Sue Boy who shipped out to the stars. They did grunt work, but they were out of Sue Boy, they got paid, and perhaps someday they could better themselves.

Not Griff.

The military refused and he was back in the Sue Boy slums, begging, stealing. It wasn't long before he fell into the service of another drug lord, this one whose lungs could tolerate Earth's air. Tere, a firecracker of a woman near Griff's age. It wasn't the drugs she flooded Astor with or the riots she started, it was the police cruiser. Her idea, all of it her idea, but who'd fired the rocket? Lights flashing at 600 meters above ground level, Griff aiming.

The recoil had knocked him back and all he saw of his work was a column of smoke, crawling skyward with the others and proclaiming rebellion from Sue Boy to Astor.

400 years. While the others cheered on the man and the woman reassembling their rifles, Griff's stomach hummed. The groans had fallen to flat hums, meek calls for sustenance. Surrender. 400 years. Griff studied the fire, the containers beyond it.

He looked over at his captors—they were huddled around the racing soldiers, blocking Griff's view—but Charlie stood apart, and Griff made eye contact with him.

Charlie came over. "What is it?"

"When might I get to eat?"

"Soon."

"Okay. I'm starving. After the long sleep, who isn't, right?"

Charlie chuckled. Uncomfortable, but genuine.

"Who won this round?"

"What?" It took Charlie a moment. "Oh, Michelle. She can put her rifle back together faster than anyone in the company."

"Impressive."

"Indeed. I'll get you some food soon."

"Thank you."

Griff offered Charlie a smile which he returned...less uncomfortable, more genuine. Charlie joined the group and Griff stared at the containers beyond the dimming fire.

There was something about the containers, echo in his memory. When the soldiers hauled him aboard the *Jefferson*, Griff had studied every detail he could before the Master Droid sealed him in his pod for the long sleep. He'd be a slave on some world untold light-years from home, but if he had his way, he wouldn't suffer for long.

The containers. With the fire dim, Griff could make out their shapes better. They were cylindrical, built to survive crashes, and covering the lid were strips of titanium, the top opened by thumbprint. Griff focused. The containers. He'd seen them before, he'd seen them the day they shoved him in his pod, the food was on the

*Jefferson*, they'd have sustenance pills for emergencies but the real foodstuffs would be on the *Jefferson*, preserved in their own long sleep and now in cylindrical containers like this, but—

Griff went cold. A flare erupted in his stomach, his heart racing, forcing a whisper out his mouth.

"Oh God."

The containers were for weapons. The same ones he'd seen before his four-century nap.

Griff studied the fire, his eyes watering less now. He catalogued what he saw and tried to get up, sliding his legs, panting. He tried to spread his arms, the binds grinding against his wrists before the absurdity of what he was doing hit him. He closed his eyes and steadied his breathing, thoughtful breath after thoughtful breath. He opened his eyes.

Another challenger faced off against the woman, the two of them disassembling their rifles to the cheers of their compatriots. The colors in the sky brightened. 400 years. Colonists, men and women released from their earthbound origins.

Griff caught Charlie's eye.

Charlie glanced at the others. The rifles ready for reassembly. Griff waited until the race started before speaking.

"There's something wrong."

"What..." The crowd cheered. "What is it?"

"The gray."

"I'm sorry?"

The crowd's cheers hit their peak. Griff said, "On the grass. There's some kind of weird gray. Right there." Griff nodded at the ground. "See it?"

Charlie bent down to examine the gray, not far enough for Griff's liking. The cheers. Little time and soon he'd have no time at all.

"Wow," Charlie said. "I think I see—"

The men of Sue Boy had taught the boys the tricks of their dangerous trade. Police binds were made of flexible steel and keylocked, but you needn't break them open. Rock back—

Griff rocked back.

—draw your knees to your chest.

Griff drew his knees to his chest.

—relax your shoulders and slid your arms free.

Griff relaxed his shoulders and slid his arms free.

—now, kick.

Griff kicked with both feet. He sent Charlie tumbling into the fire, where he screamed and rolled through the embers and the flames. The flames caught the stunner hooked to his belt.

The explosion of equipment screeched on this alien world and it was background noise to Griff.

He fled into the forest.

\* \* \*

Griff ran at a staggered pace, tilting from side to side like a punching bag. He inched toward collapse and set his head against a tree, eyes closed, thinking not of Charlie on the fire or what he saw in its flames, but of the day he got arrested. They'd celebrated afterwards. A police cruiser down, all the pigs onboard dead on impact. The scraps they fashion into weapons and what's best, it told Astor cops that Sue Boy, the slums society had ostracized them into, was theirs. It belonged to people like Griff. The rocket. Her idea. Yes, but who'd fired it, and Griff whispered, "Four hundred years."

The tears stung his eyes and they meandered along his cheeks. Griff took a breath and cried.

\* \* \*

Tottering beneath the watch of the turtleshell leaves. Bound man, haggard, starving. He moaned. He'd never known there could be hunger so terrible and when he heard movement he rushed toward it, certain it was the horned rabbit or some other animal native to this world.

He saw nothing and later collapsed.

\* \* \*

Awake under the kaleidoscope of colors. Dimmer here. Day and night on this world. What did the colonists think they knew about this planet? Griff rolled over in the grass, spitting dirt. He pushed himself up with his bound hands and moaned as a hunger pang swept through his gut.

It was slow going on his feet and he stumbled through the woods. The denizens of Sue Boy. Theirs was a victory that was short-lived; the cops got them. One by one they all fell, and no plea could spare Griff. Earth did not execute her condemned like in ancient times. Now they slaved—now they starved, and when Griff heard the command to Halt, he broke off into a staggering dash.

He made it a few feet before tripping. He planted flat on his face and spitting dirt from his mouth, Griff caught a glimpse of the glass blades, all gray, before a boot kicked him over onto his back.

Griff stared up at the turtleshell leaves and their wonderlands of color. The figure stepped over him and as Griff blinked, Roderick's stone face cleared between two turtleshell leaves.

"You didn't get far." Roderick grabbed Griff by his binds. The binds dug into his wrists but Griff was too famished to wince. Roderick marched Griff to the other soldiers who now stood eight in number, their rifles slung along their backs.

"I want two pipes on him at all times," Roderick said.

The women who'd been assembling her rifle earlier spoke up: "Why not waste him now?"

"We'll..." And the first sign of hesitation Griff had seen on Roderick cracked his stone face. He closed his eyes and opening them said, "Move out."

The two soldiers holding Griff had rough grips. Two behind him, rifles ready. Men on the outside of the formation with their rifles, Roderick at the front, leading them through the woods.

They did not stop. Day or night, the kaleidoscope of colors waxed and waned. Griff's feet ached. The hunger pangs and a hollow burp crawled up his throat and popped somewhere south of his tongue.

Execution here, or execution at their unknown destination, it no longer mattered to Griff. There would be no official colony here. Other slaves had likely gotten free, same as him, and perhaps they could found their own colony. Even the surviving colonists waking up from their pods, perhaps they would unite and the next arrival in four hundred years would find a flourishing civilization and spotting the gray mountain, Griff stopped in his tracks with his captors.

Films in ancient times lacked color. Griff had seen pictures of such scenes, and that was the only way his mind could make sense of what he saw. Gray, like

*the grass blades*

the films, the mountain lacked color, it lacked definition.

It lacked life.

"Jackson," Roderick said. "Where's the ship?"

"Straight ahead," said a young man barely out of his teens. He stood near the front, commpad cupped in his hands. Catching Roderick's look, he added, "That's where the signal's coming from."

Roderick unhooked a farviewer from his belt. He gazed through the digital lens at the mountain, lowered the farviewer and gazed again. When he lowered it for a second time, he said, "Straight ahead?"

"Yes sir," Jackson said.

Roderick growled, and Griff watched worry crack his stone face. A human like everyone else.

"Sir?" said the woman. "Sir?"

Roderick went on staring at the mountain. Then he composed himself and said, "Move out."

\* \* \*

More of the gray area came into view as they marched toward the ship. It wasn't just one mountain, it was a range, and downhill led to forests leeched of color and life, the sky itself gray and the border between the kaleidoscope of colors and the gray shimmering with a heavenly glow.

Facing the mountains was a temple.

Untouched by the gray. Made from the same stone you'd find on Earth. A cap covered the templetop and a lone rod pointed skyward like a weathervane. It overlooked the gray area and Roderick ordered everyone to the temple.

They formed up on the side of it, overlooking the gray area, and the sight was unmistakable: the wreckage of the *Jefferson*.

Descent through the atmosphere had stripped the *Jefferson* of most of its hull, leaving skeletal remains. A mighty vessel constructed by Nang Shipyards in orbit around Mars, it lay in the gray area a defeated husk of itself.

The gray crawled over the *Jefferson* like kudzu vines.

Griff swayed, his eyes burning. Ahead, Roderick dropped to one knee again and surveyed the ship, the farviewer humming as he zoomed in.

"Move in."

Roderick rose and hooked the farviewer back to his belt and the others stared at him, their rifles no longer trained on Griff. Doubt broke through on Roderick's face again, and he turned, surveying everyone, his eyes landing on Griff and now his face was completely broken.

"You," Roderick whispered. He swallowed. "You're enjoying this, aren't you? The worst our species has to offer, you should have been executed." Roderick's eyes watered, his hand creeping to his rifle. "You're scum, you're worthless. You don't deserve to found civilization on a new planet. Did you know what we had planned for our slaves? You see, it's not as simple as working you to death. First we work you for a year. Then we put you back in the long sleep for five years. Then we work you for two. Then five more years.

"Your labor will outlive me, and by the end, you'll be broken, and no thoughts will pass through that thick skull of yours other than those of work."

He branded *work* with a growl and trained his rifle on Griff.

Griff stared at him.

Roderick lowered the rifle, a grin of crooked teeth warping his face. "I have a better idea.

"Send him into the temple."

The soldiers near Griff didn't move. Roderick repeated himself, shouting, his voice cracking and the soldiers grabbed Griff's arms and marched him to the temple.

A bird was etched into the stone above the doorway, its wings pointed in opposite directions and its beak open. A tongue flailed out from its beak, thin, lesser birds etched around it in liftoff. The soldiers marched Griff inside, hesitating, and then they let go of him.

Sealed in glass tubes were people. They lay on their backs, hands clasped at their waists and they were in color. They breathed with life, beamed with beauty. They were all naked and dials beside the tubes blinked with the same kaleidoscope of colors Griff had seen in the sky and in the turtleshell leaves.

The soldiers stopped at different pods while Griff went ahead. And when he spotted himself in a pod, he looked down at his feet. He raised his right foot.

A spiral of gray curled across the sole of his foot, from his heel to his toes.

Griff dropped down, pressing the back of his head against the glass tube. His vision changed, color leaving the world, and the commotion outside meant little to him. Neither did the blasts of the rifles. Griff closed his eyes, his hunger pangs fading.

The gray took care of it.

# And So Down the Drain
## Eric Del Carlo

There were still low places: the chilly sophistications of the galaxy notwithstanding and regardless of the munificence which was custom, and often policy, on the myriad human-settled worlds. And despite the fact that a person could only truly falter in this halcyon time when they chose, explicitly, to fail.

Karstens would argue—if any were to challenge him—that choice had been ripped savagely from him. He was not like others; and others were not like he. Once, he had shared this fantastic distinction with the one being in the universe who understood it. But that one, his twin telepathic brother, no longer lived. And it was this impossibly tragic death which accounted for Karstens' grand downfall.

He arrived at the Drain in the perpetual dusk. The first moment of jumpdown told him he was somewhere...*else*. Even ahead of his disembarkation from the colorless, utile craft, the unkempt mood of the place seeped in and found him. His innards twinged, and his heart seemed to speed and slow all at once. When the hatch slid back, he was a wavering, off-balance figure. His lone travel bag, of red fabric, dropped to his feet. He almost left it there and walked out to face his new environment, but that would have been too melodramatic. His brother would have called him on it, immediately, no matter where he was; snickering through their special psychic link, deflating the theatricality of the moment.

But Bristol said nothing, because Bristol was no more. Karstens bent to retrieve his luggage, and staggered off onto the arrivals platform.

The Drain, as this world was called, had its habitation underground, which explained the endless twilight. Only so much effort was made toward lighting the interweaving, interconnecting warrens. It wasn't that the world was poor; "poor" was an outmoded concept. But the will didn't exist here for a municipal undertaking of any real magnitude. The Drain had its caves. The Drain had breathable underground air. The world had all the necessary accommodations to call itself civilized without having taken on the busy trappings of luxury and elegance that adorned so many other places throughout the galaxy. Karstens had seen such places, had dwelled there at the highest levels, among the privileged classes. He and Bristol...yes, he and Bristol had known that lavishness; and yet it had all been game. They were the mercurial pair, the mirror opposite twins: so perfectly the same in their physical appearance, so apart in disposition. Introvert and extrovert. And yet between them such connectivity, such accord. Such...say it! say it!...such love.

And now there was emptiness, and Karstens, accordingly, had come to an empty place. A mean subterranean world, a hole in the ground. The low place. One of the few genuinely low places in the galaxy.

He stepped off the gray slate of the platform, in the murky light, to go find the room he had arranged.

\* \* \*

His lodgings weren't dingy. The furnishings and fixtures were solid, the chamber clean, the devices functional. In fact, this room could have been dropped onto worlds like Abgrund or Mortaja or dozens of others and no traveler would think a negative thought about it. It was only that the climate of the Drain leaked in here, or perhaps Karstens had carried it in on his person, like a scent, like a light coating of greasy mist.

And so the yellow patterned bedding seemed leached of its cheerful hue. And the walls felt tired as they pressed in.

Karstens went out to face his new world. Let his failure truly commence.

The enormous cave system was a natural formation, and humans had laid their structures and byways and lighting and other infrastructure along the existing lines. This was common architectural practice in the galaxy. An organic approach was the norm, blending habitations into local nature, thereby not seriously interrupting the native flow. In this way such wonders as the Emerald Volcano on Mappemonde and the Quartz Falls on Volna remained preserved. Karstens had seen these splendid sights and many more. He and Bristol both had witnessed them, sometimes only through the agency of their telepathic bond. Over the years they had rarely been in the same place at the same time. It hadn't been necessary that they be.

As Karstens plodded along a raised walkway, with the soaring cavern roof overhead, it felt to him that this place—the Drain—had failed to insinuate itself properly into the environment. Its strangely mean buildings appeared jammed into position, forcefully, as if in constructing this settlement a violation had occurred rather than a mediation. Yet he couldn't point to a single feature of his surroundings that supported this glum impression.

Nevertheless, he availed himself of the local amenities. He ate at an eatery; he had no intention of starving himself. Mineral dust collected into artful motifs had been sprayed and laminated onto the interior walls. After, he walked more. Those mineral veins were starkly visible on the rough walls which rose all around. He had visited worlds before where one never saw a sun, even underground habitations like this. But he had never known anywhere to be so...*sullen*.

He spoke to no one, but plenty of people were about. They seemed engaged in the normal tasks of daily life everywhere, but there was a desultory taint to all activities, as if these inhabitants had to push themselves into each individual action, as though they would rather just languish and do nothing, except maybe brood.

Of course, he considered the possibility that all these observations weren't really directed outward, but *in*. After all, he had been the introvert of the twin sibling duo. He was the ponderer, the muser. He was comfortable asking the slow questions of the universe and expecting little in the way of a reply. Not that he had been unhappy. Far from it. Life had been an adventure, a joy even; but what had made it so, in part, was the everlasting presence of Bristol. Always at his elbow, forever in his head, the intensely familiar fellowship, the extravagant intimacy.

He paused now in his wanderings, looking around almost angrily. He had come to the Drain to initiate his final decline. His living self had been hollowed out. He was a husk. He was a psychic with no one to receive his thoughts; nor were there any outside transmissions to welcome into his brain. It stood, to his reckoning, that this world, the Drain, should candidly reflect his inner turmoil. It should be something far worse than a mere drab milieu. It ought to be decrepit, despicable, a seething junk heap populated by other broken individuals limping about in sackcloth and ashes. The Drain had its reputation. It was a *low place*! It was why he had come.

"Now," said a voice nearby, "that's a new face if ever I have seen one."

He turned—spun, really. But the woman stood a reasonable distance away, not directly behind him as it had seemed just a second ago. There was no doubt she had addressed him: light blue eyes were fastened on him, and the crooked smile on her lips felt aimed his way. She was relatively trim, groomed nonchalantly, clothing of no particular cut or insistent color. Comely? No. Physically intriguing? Perhaps. But he hadn't come to this world to seek new lovers. Really, he didn't care if he ever had intercourse again.

"New?" he said; then: "Face?" These were inanities. But she was intruding.

Her smile—if that was what it was—became even further lopsided, then disappeared altogether as her eyes suddenly glinted.

"It's not an insult, and I'm not here to haze you. People do come to the Drain, but it's not all that often, or rare for that matter. It's just...an occurrence. And since you're occurring right in front of me, I thought I would note it. Hello."

"Hello."

"You look like you could use a meal."

"I just ate."

"An active metabolism, then. The new face. Ah, yes. I'll explain. It's the look of effrontery, like this world has slapped you hard."

"I don't—" he started to say, but she had it right.

"The Drain isn't what you thought. Or wanted. Or thought you wanted." She appeared to find this briefly amusing. The crooked smile flickered again.

He gathered thought. He gathered breath. Then wondered why he was bothering to try to answer this woman.

Her blue eyes glinted with greater intensity, like the diamond pits on Akarui. "Want to flip with me?"

"I'm not interested in sex," he said.

\* \* \*

Flipping wasn't sex. It was the word for a popular local opiate. It wasn't grown on this world, nor even processed here; but it found its way to the Drain in large quantities, where it was consumed by a widespread subculture. The woman—her name was Dania—took Karstens into this realm and initiated him into its mysteries. He went willingly, but without enthusiasm. He wasn't terribly curious what the drug would do, and wasn't especially surprised by its mind-altering effects. He didn't see the face of God nor look for it. Flip had a severe addictive bite, but he would sometimes forgo his next dose just to experience the bitter withdrawal. On other worlds, in richer circumstances, he had known other exotic narcotics, ones that let you believe you were kissing a star or breathing deeply of the black's unthinkably cold vacuum. These were the mind-toys of the elite. The brain's synapses were mechanisms to be casually diddled by potent substances which would swing you through the whole of the universe and land you right back on your feet.

So he didn't become a hopeless flip addict. Dania appeared to find this, too, amusing. She herself was a habitual user. The two of them spent time together, not all of it in the throes of the favored local opiate. Part of him appreciated her introducing him to the Drain's underside. This somewhat seedy sect was closer to what he had anticipated finding on this world, but even this was something of a letdown. The degradation wasn't sufficient; the sleaziness didn't reach as deep as it should; it just wasn't...enough.

Sex still didn't matter to him. Neither did eating or sleeping, for that matter. But he saw to his necessities anyway. He continued to live in his room, and very little was asked of him. If he wished to flip all day and night, he could; and the Drain would simply carry him along.

Once, sex had been very engaging. The true stuff of life. The first time he and his brother had shared a lover they had been sixteen. They had passed a dazed, dreamy-eyed boy back and forth between them; seducing, spurning, sending off to the other, taking back, re-seducing...It had all been rather comical. Those fleshy bouts had certainly been imbued with a base delight. But it was as much—or more—the re-experiencing through the other's senses which truly enflamed. Being inside Bristol's skull while he did lovely lewd things to that boy was an unspeakable joy. Every sensation was doubled. Every ecstasy increased exponentially. Karstens felt not just the physical pleasure again but his sibling's delight; and more, Bristol's delight over *Karsten's* delight, a glorious feedbacking loop, going round and round.

In the years that had followed there had been legions of women, scores of men. Beds in sumptuous palaces, piled deep with writhing bodies, and one or the other of the telepathic brothers in the carnal mix. One there...and one elsewhere; but both men feeling, knowing, experiencing on the most intimate level.

Yes. Yes. Hedonistic glories. Sexual raptures. But they two had also been about their business, a serious trade it was, too. The two identical brothers, one inwardly turned, the other with an external temperament. Each had infiltrated select echelons, exclusive precincts of galactic society. Not everyone could get in here. Almost nobody could, in fact. These were realms of gamblers, of adventurers in dark entertainments, outsized extroverted personalities bent on blazing a way onto the fabric of the galaxy. These, naturally, were Bristol's prey. He could go among the daredevils and the death-grinning eccentrics, he could perform his chaste seductions—and sometimes not so chaste—and learn the inner secrets of these cabals. He was never apprehended as a spy, even though those reaches were jealously guarded by the highest security imaginable. No surveillance devices were ever found on him; there were none; none was needed. Everything he experienced his twin knew, instantly, in full detail, no matter what physical distance stood between them. In this way, activities were reported on in real time.

And Karstens, consequently, could through the wiles of his own introverted personality quietly intrude on those clandestine places where arcane scientists and researchers and even artists met and conferred, where the best untamed minds let their ideas off all restraints. Karstens could move among them, could glean vital information for the agencies of galactic government. This was a critical service. But to Karstens and his brother it was in the end just a game.

They were unique. They were secretly celebrated by those bureaus and covert state departments which made use of them. Naturally, they were rewarded; but what did that matter? What was wealth any longer?

Grand times. The best. No amount of jumpspace could separate the twins. Both brothers knew they could stand at opposite ends of the immense galaxy and hear and send and mingle their thoughts as if they were lounging in the same room. Their singular gift was like no other; *they* were like no others.

Nothing could part them. Nothing—

He flipped hard that night, those ethereal nights in the Drain which were little different from days. He went through until dawn, then past it, into the new day, approaching another night...

Dania was there. She hadn't been before. She liked a flipping partner, someone to blather drug-addled nonsense at. But he had been alone last night. What—

"Come on." She was tugging on him. A moment ago, he realized belatedly, she had been mopping his face with a steaming cloth. He tried to squirm away, muttering that he had only been flipping for a day. "Wrong. You're going into your third day. Get up, Karstens. Come. We're going upside. Get up!"

It seemed like a fragment of opiate dreaming, some pointless bit of busyness. But he let himself be shaken from his unusually deep stupor, cooperated bemusedly with getting cleaned up and dressed. Then he found himself indeed be led "upside"; this was the way to the surface of the world, a world where life abided only underground. He remained amused and mildly perplexed as the elevator took them up, he but went along. There were environment suits to seal into, a custodian at the airlock. Karstens had sobered considerably. Dania had slapped a patch on his neck without asking permission; it stung a little, but he felt his arteries throbbing pleasantly, the passageways being cleansed of recreational contaminants.

"Let's go outside." Her voice was soft on the suit radio. Her gloved hand took his, and they stepped out, together.

It was some kind of ammonia tundra, shreds of icy debris being borne along by a fierce wind. The dense sky was green, and the surface was greenish and bluish, with unimaginative mountainous formations in the distance. Lifeless. Vastly inhospitable. But...not unbeautiful, he thought, now that his thoughts were returning and finding a steady speed. He looked around slowly.

"It's peaceful," he murmured, forgetting momentarily that he was transmitting.

Dania came back over the radio immediately: "Yes." She squeezed his hand, and he turned to gaze at her through her helmet plate. Her eyes looked a bit hollow, but color dotted her cheeks. He wondered when she had last flipped. Not today, he felt sure.

"You never did tell me," she said, and there was more of a twinkle than a glint in her eyes. Her smile even looked sincere, not that he minded her crooked one.

"Tell you what, Dania?"

"Your tragic story. If you wanted to, this would be a good time. And I will listen. I will listen." This last had the tenor of an oath. He realized that this was perhaps something of a ceremony on this world, like his baptism into the cult of flipping; but this, maybe, was something more important. He understood her meaning: what tragedy had brought him here? This was the Drain. One didn't choose to journey here on a whim or out of simple curiosity. Only the genuinely damaged were welcome.

He let out a long breath.

He told her. It was the first time he had related the facts in such stark continuous detail. He didn't quite know what he felt afterward—breathless? a bit dizzy?—but he didn't feel worse than before. And now someone else in the universe had the truth of Bristol in her memory; his brother would not simply vanish were something to happen to Karstens.

But what *would* happen to him, on this world? What was the Drain to give him, ultimately?

Dania still held his hand. After a long silence she said, "Maybe you should go to the Drain."

A wry smile flickered across his lips. "I'm on the Drain."

"No. The actual Drain." He didn't understand. She started to elaborate, then, realizing, stopped with a soft gasp. "You don't know, do you? This world is called what it is for a reason. It's named for the Drain itself, the ancient artifact, the...the portal or whatever it is....Karstens? You *don't know*?"

Her incredulity both annoyed and intrigued him. He was dismayed to learn that the artifact she spoke of was indeed here and quite well known; famous—or infamous—in fact, in the way of the arcane accoutrements of the ancients which were to be found scattered about the galaxy. The Milky Way of course teemed with life, with cultures and star-faring civilizations...only, these empires almost never overlapped. Galactic time was epochal. It was meted out in self-contained eternities. Mighty domains rose, flourished, abided, then fell. They might dominate for millennia before relinquishing their grip on the stars. Humankind, too, would get its share of eons; then, so said the wisest heads, it would crash and disintegrate, like all the others. But that was a worry for tomorrows unimaginably distant from now.

Karstens, in his lavish travels, had seen a few of these relics. It was the ones which still had a little juice in them—some operating power—that drew the most interest, of course. The Face of Chance. The Chanting Whirlpool, on Tumanako. The Standstill Gaze on Ológbò, where the unspeakably old machine still froze reality around you, allowing one to see the arrested heart of the universe in mid-beat.

Dania, once he had recovered himself a bit more, took him to see the Drain.

\* \* \*

He thought at first it was merely a pool of mercury. It appeared reflective, but dense and somewhat distorted; surrounding it was a raised brim of what he initially mistook for natural stone. But as he studied the artifact further, he saw that the encircling brink was some curious *living* substance, or at least something silicate-like which subtly pulsed as if with internal life.

The Drain itself—that was, the circular pool at the center of the cavern which immediately drew the eye—was nine meters or so across. He thought it unremarkable. The surface didn't even ripple. He was forming some droll comment for Dania who stood at his left and half a step behind, when he experienced the pull. It was an elusive tug, easy to dismiss initially; after all, he had over-flipped recently—no point in denying it—a minor misadventure he put down to dwelling too intently on his brother's tragic absence. Not that such brooding could be helped. Not that he *should* feel obliged to downplay in any way the terrible —

It was a tickle, a twinge, deep inside his head. He couldn't pin down the sensation...and some instinctive part of him was afraid to do so. Yet fear wasn't what he really felt. This was—this was something familiar? It grazed a memory cluster, some dormant reflex perhaps.

Dania gave a sniff, to the left and just behind, out of his sight. "Everybody feels that draw."

She had spoken gently, but he wanted to turn and tell her to shut up. He didn't, though. It was quite possible he would have spent much more time on this world without knowing its open secret, the presence of this ancient artifact, if she hadn't told him. And Dania, in her way, had been kind to him. Like him, she was surely damaged. There seemed to be pieces missing from her. Should he ask her her story, as she'd asked for his?

The pull didn't intensify, but it came into sharper mental focus. Then he realized, with a soul-jarring start, why it was familiar. Those receptors in his brain, so long unused now...A sound escaped him, a low mewl of pain or wonder or horror.

The Drain was reaching him on the same psychic wavelength he and his twin had shared all their lives.

\* \* \*

It sent him into a new kind of turmoil. This was a different upheaval from that which had utterly overtaken him when he had learned about—experienced, *felt*— Bristol's death. Then he was shattered, nothing left but fragments; and he, Karstens, was left to scrabble about like a wounded animal trying to scoop its disemboweled insides back within the casing of its flesh.

Now, "hearing" a whisper on that special frequency —it was...God! it was like madness and marvel, a punch to the center of his sick soul. He didn't know whether to gibber with delight or wail as if for the demise of the universe. Neither reaction befitted him. He was, after all, the quiet one, the inward creature. He noted things, absorbed them, drew unhurried conclusions. It was why the cerebral cliques had welcomed him in when he was engaged in the espionage business with his brother.

He barely slept. He ate when he remembered to, but this wasn't dismal self-neglect; he was preoccupied, this discovery crowding out all else. In his clean yet ineffably shabby room he researched the Drain on the archival outlet that came with his lodgings. The artifact was located at a distant terminus of snaking grottos. Sites such as it understandably drew keen archeological interest, and the Drain had been thoroughly studied, for what those studies were worth. Lots of inconclusive data; that was the norm. These ancient star-spanning empires had used awesome technology. But it was, perhaps, no less impressive than what human beings had devised. Maybe the set of ancients who had constructed the Drain had gotten about the galaxy by hopping in and out of wormholes. It might be that, were the tables reversed, they would find human jump drives just as majestic and baffling.

He had stopped flipping altogether. Dania came to him a few times, seeking a recreational partner, but he turned her away. Only after she had gone did he realize he'd neglected once again to ask about her tragedy. He hoped vaguely that this wasn't some awful faux pas on his part.

What was the Drain? What could it do?

The pull—the *draw*, Dania had called it—was well documented, but not quantified. This didn't surprise Karstens. When he and Bristol had gone to work for the government bureaus, specialists descended upon them, and scanned them and performed their occult tests, and found nothing they could safely measure. The telepathic link was beyond evaluation. The twins already knew this. Never in their lives had they encountered another pair like themselves.

But the statistic which leaped out at him with a shocking bluntness was the suicide rate associated with the artifact/phenomenon. Apparently for many years now people had been jumping into the Drain. Jumping! Just climbing up on the brim and taking a dive into that mirrored surface, which evidently was not a solid sheet but something that gave, like—his original impression again—a pool full of mercury. Anyone who made such a dive simply disappeared, forever. The pool closed over the intrusion and left no ripple, and that was that. No scanning showed any trace of the person, who was officially listed as a suicide.

It shook Karstens. People came to this world bearing their hurts. Like him, they had sought a low place, so to salt their own wounds. And some, so said the documentation, chose to end their suffering by leaping into the very maw of an unknown, perhaps incomprehensible curio left over from an age before the Earth itself had finished cooling. Incredible.

Incredible. But—understandable?

This knowledge wrested him away from his monkish research. He went back out into the tireless twilight. He visited establishments he'd patronized; he went into the dens where Dania had taken him flipping. Employing his old introverted charm, he plied local characters with questions. Did they personally know anyone who had taken a dive into the Drain? People assumed Karstens himself was thinking about making the leap. He could see the assessment in their eyes. But no one tried to talk him out of it. A few did, however, give him a few scraps of information. The incidents were true. The Drain took its supplicants, one after the next; in dribs, in spurts; and whether these were genuine suicides or something else, they didn't say. Karstens pondered that *something else*, and eventually understood that some believed the Drain to be a gateway. That to leap down and through was to pass into another realm. That some wondrous, beatific, divine encounter awaited on the other side. That was draw, the pull, one chronic flipper said with a seamed and seamy smile: "Those the angels, whispering to you…"

Karstens searched around. He counted heads, noted faces. Some people who had been on the scene when he had arrived now appeared gone. It chilled him, but kindled something in him as well, a strange livid thing, with its own dark heat and a flat unflinching shine to it.

He had to visit the Drain again.

\* \* \*

Today he was not the only visitor. A woman—older, striking, beautiful in fact—stood on the other side of the beguiling reflection pool. He hesitated before stepping all the way into the cavern; but the woman's gaze lethargically lifted, passed over him, and drifted away.

He took up a place opposite her. Again he felt the pull, and this time it was immediately apparent that his old telepathic receptors were being touched. This should be Bristol's voice! But his brother didn't speak, nor did the familiar loving in-rush of feeling come, Bristol's extroverted charisma, his braying psychic laugh. Nothing. Just a static buzz, like a communication channel open but unused.

His eyes fell to the pool. He examined the surface. It dully reflected the striated cavern roof. This site was some distance from the habitations; visitors reached it by driving little carts along a lengthy narrow roadway. The woman's cart was already here when he arrived. He found himself distracted by her. At first this irritated him. He'd come here to—meditate? to study?—to be alone with the Drain. The woman didn't speak and did nothing to further acknowledge his presence, not even a follow-up glance. Yet in the cavern's sensitive acoustics he fancied he could hear her breathing. But none of this, he eventually realized, was what bothered him. He *recognized* this person. She was...famous. Yes. A singer, with a voice as rich and resonant as time and fate. She had performed great operatic exhibitions. A woman known across the worlds. But—she had dropped out of sight, at the peak of her eminence. And now she was here, looking listlessly into an ancient artifact where people traditionally threw themselves when they'd had enough of their lives.

A strange stab of pity pierced him. But what, truly, was *he* doing here if not the same thing? Thinking of taking a leap. Pondering a dive down the Drain. Or was he ludicrously hoping to hear his dead sibling's voice come through on its old wavelength?

His coming here today was a stupid gesture. Bristol would laugh. Should laugh. Or Karstens should laugh at himself.

He turned on his heel and left the pool and its bewitching pulling effect behind.

\* \* \*

The nightmare needed no embellishing: it was a straightforward narrative. A mental retelling of the moment when his twin had died. Karstens had been speaking with Bristol, telepathic conversation using actual words and phrases and sentences and pauses, like verbal discourse. They did this sometimes—rather than merely and adroitly passing images back and forth to each other—to keep in practice. And to amuse themselves. Much had been amusing back then.

Karstens had been in a lounge, one with cool mahogany lines and firm leather furniture. Bristol was on another world, a soupy tropical place he said; lots of prehistoric foliage and fragrant oceans of mud. He was having a delightful time. The brothers were between spying assignments.

*What sort of food do they have?* Karstens asked.

*Sautéed insects, big as your fist. The wine is ghastly.* This was Bristol, enjoying himself, reveling in all experiences, all adversities.

*What is—* Karstens started to say, swirling the contents of his own glass in the lounge. But in that instant it happened. The mishap. The terrible event. It was a stupid thing which had occurred. The universe, it seemed, was full of stupidities. A seismic jolt of considerable assertiveness had struck virtually below Bristol's feet, and the roof of the hotel he was staying at came loose from its supports in detrimental chunks, and one of these crushed him. Instantaneous death. Not even enough time to have fully registered the temblor underfoot.

Karstens came out of the nightmare lacquered with sweat, immediately aware of his room and its bled-dry colors; and an impulse seized him. His hands shook as he dressed. He went out into the underground night. And sought Dania, in her own quarters. He had never been inside before. She came to her door in filmy sleeping attire, and took his hands, and drew him in. He didn't tell her his dream. He had already explained how his brother had died, which was his tragic story—or was it Bristol's tragedy? Instead, he asked for her tale.

She didn't seem to mind having had her sleep disturbed. She didn't appear to be flipping; she was alone.

Her decor was far more personal than his as if she'd been here considerably longer than he, with tchotchkes and wall hangings, and a whispery atmosphere of aromatic weariness in the rooms. Her story, which she told in a steady drip of words, was one of heartbreak. Death had not been involved, only the death of love, which had been sufficient to bring her to the Drain. Karstens listened intently, without comment. He only truly became aware of her flimsy state of dress when she crossed her arms over her breasts.

After she finished speaking, they went to her bed and pantomimed their way through a session of lovemaking. As she shuddered against him, a brittle happiness radiated from her; when the pleasure ebbed, the joy didn't immediately disappear, but it thinned as he watched her, their bodies cooling. She smiled crookedly. He thumbed a tear off his cheek, one he was unaware of producing, kissed her briefly on the lips, and went out.

\* \* \*

He slept again, dreamlessly, and woke refreshed. A peculiar optimism was with him through his morning ablutions. He decided to seek out Dania once more, this time for a meal. He'd eaten with no one since arriving here.

There was commotion on the byways and in the handful of cafes he passed. He stopped to inquire. No one said anything when someone dived into the Drain; that, simply, was not the stuff of gossip, it being too private and poignant an event. But *this*—

He hurried along. His pulse was quick. He felt it thumping at his wrist, his throat, his temples. He reached the elevator and went up. He got as far as the airlock. The custodian had been joined by a phalanx of uniformed individuals. Everyone looked grim, but no urgency charged the scene. What had happened was done; this was the necessary bureaucratic mop-up.

She had gone out in an environment suit, but she had shed its protection once outside, after walking a fair distance across the greenish, bluish ice. There was no ambiguity about this death: unlike those who chose the Drain, this act was quite definitely a suicide....

Karstens drove the small buzzy cart at a reckless speed. No one was on the track ahead or behind him. He came to the cavern somehow without wiping out into the irregular, mineral-striped walls. He staggered out and toward the Drain, kicking away his shoes. The cavern too was empty. Perhaps the famous singer had taken her leap, perhaps not. With bare feet he climbed onto the lip of the pool. The strange, living rock-like material palpitated the naked soles of his feet. His toes gripped. His knees bent. The empty pull of the pool sang in his head, promising nothing but enticing him nonetheless. He was aware of sounds coming from himself, more wordless mewls, animal noises almost. He was done talking. Done listening. Done *being*...This was the only way forward now.

Muscles tensed throughout him. His eyes narrowed. He crouched lower, and then he sprang, and went up and hit his apex, and came down in a smooth arc, and saw his face—and Bristol's face, precisely the same—in the distortion of the reflection—

And so.

Down through the Drain.

\* \* \*

The skin of mercury that was the pool's surface closed above him. But...he was aware. He was conscious! He had expected instant immolation, a complete and immediate halt to his reality. Instead he was sinking down through some unknowable substance, fantastically strange sensations tearing at every part of him. He couldn't see—yet he could! Kaleidoscopic mayhem poured into his eyes, and heat and cold and love and lunacy caressed his flesh, his being; he might not even *have* flesh anymore, and it didn't matter—

He wanted to cry out, in terror, in ecstasy. Instead, he threw words ahead of himself, into the baffling abyss which lay before him, the wonder of a reality that was no reality at all.

*What sort of food do they have?* he cried.

And somewhere in the forward distance Bristol's braying laughter answered.

# Gunships over Ganymede
## Lee Clark Zumpe

Gunships over Ganymede,
their vigilant crews scanning the sector,
expecting an armada of alien battlecruisers
that never materialize.

Terra-formers over Titan,
engineering a more suitable atmosphere,
reformatting surface topography,
and stimulating a flourishing milieu.

Colony transports over Callisto,
populating floating city-states,
and underwater complexes
in seas teeming with transplanted halophiles.

Spaceliners over lonely Sedna,
far-flung trans-Neptunian object,
humanity's solitary outpost overlooking
the Oort Cloud and interstellar space.

## Who?

**Lauren McBride** finds inspiration in faith, family, nature, science, and membership in the SFPA. She enjoys swimming, gardening, baking, reading, writing, and knitting scarves for our troops.

**Jason Lairamore** is a writer of science fiction, fantasy, and horror who lives in Oklahoma with his beautiful wife and their three monstrously marvelous children. He is a 2024 *Jim Baen Memorial Award* finalist and a 2023 *Baen Fantasy Adventure Award* finalist. He has won *Writer of the Future* honors with sixteen honorable mentions, one silver honorable mention, and a semi-finalist placement.

**James Arthur Anderson** says: I am currently Professor Emeritus at Johnson & Wales University and a part-time English instructor at East Georgia State College.

Eric Del Carlo's fiction has appeared in Analog, Asimov's, Clarkesworld and many other publications over the years. He makes his home in his native California."

www.ingramcontent.com/pod-product-compliance
Lightning Source LLC
LaVergne TN
LVHW012030060526
838201LV00061B/4542